DEATH ON THE

A thriller by

Jago Hayden

**Published by Black Lion Books,
Crannoge Boy, Loughros Point, Ardara, Co. Donegal, Ireland**

PUBLISHED 2003

ISBN 0-9539372-1-6

All rights reserved. No part of this publication may be reproduced, stored in a retrieval system, or transmitted in any form or by any means, electronic, mechanical, photocopying, recording or otherwise, in any way without the prior permission of the publisher, except for criticism or review.

© Copyright 2003

Enquiries to:

Black Lion Books,
Crannoge Boy, Loughros Point, Ardara, Co. Donegal.
Telephone: +353-(0)74-9541215   E-mail: jagohayden@eircom.net

Printed by:
eprint limited
105 Lagan Road, Dublin Industrial Estate, Glasnevin, Dublin 11.
Telephone: +353-(0)1-830 4141   Fax: +353-(0)1-830 4218
E-mail: books@eprint.ie   Web: www.eprint.ie

Cover design and illustration by Kevin Hayden

Portrait of author by Donnelly Studios, Donegal

DEDICATION

To all who make their living from the sea.

A work of fiction

This novel is a work of fiction in its entirety. The characters portrayed in it are unique, and are not intended to bear any resemblance to any real person, living or dead. The events depicted are imaginary. That said, the work draws on the very real conflict in Northern Ireland, and the remarkable developments in Irish fishing since the 1980's, for its ambience.

It is true that in the 1980's, Irish fishermen were the world masters of the technique of pair-midwater trawling. It is true that they regularly took bags of fish in excess of 800 tons. It is true that trawlers were towed under by nuclear submarines. It is a fact that the largest and most powerful trawler afloat in the world today is owned by an Irishman.

There is no doubt that soldiers of the British Army shot civilians on the streets of Londonderry, and ascertaining the full truth of that matter is currently the business of the Saville Inquiry. It is equally true that innocent people were murdered by 'paramilitaries' on all sides of the divide, and their bodies never found.

It has been my fantasy to combine elements similar to all of these in a work of fiction, to entertain and inform. I hope my readers enjoy it.

J.H

FOREWORD

It takes someone with an understanding of the sea to write about life aboard a modern fishing trawler working the deep edge of the North Atlantic shelf – one of the most unforgiving environments on the planet. Someone who has been there himself. Someone who knows what it takes to survive in an industry that is deemed to be one of the most dangerous in the world. Jago Hayden is such a one.

As a young man starting his career in the fledgling Irish fishing industry, he spent time on fishery research vessels in Ireland and Scotland, before moving on to spend a number of years as a fisheries development officer in East Africa. On his return to Ireland, he quickly found his way back into the sea-related sector and eventually became managing director of Swan Net Ltd., a Killybegs-based company involved in the design and manufacture of fishing gear for the world market. It was in this role that Jago Hayden – better known to his customers as Seamus – became one of the best-known figures in the industry, travelling to all corners of the world and building up a vast knowledge of fishing on a global scale.

During that period, there was a tremendous change in the industry in Ireland. Within the space of just a few years, the Irish pelagic fleet developed into one of the most modern in Europe. The harbour in Killybegs from which Jago worked, boasted some of the most technically-advanced vessels ever built for the fishing industry. His daily contact with them gave him an intimate knowledge of their fishing operations, and an understanding of the business, which few could match.

It is against this background that he has set the action of *Death on the Deep Edge*. He dared imagine, even in 1985, that Ireland might possess "the most powerful trawler afloat", and he has built a story of intrigue and drama that takes us from the Cold War through the cold Atlantic Ocean to even colder prison cells. Colder still, the bitter issue of the 'disappeared' in the conflict in Northern Ireland. And if his characters take occasional comfort between times in this warm bed or that…..

This is a work of fiction. But it is true-to-life.

Martin Howley,
Skipper and co-owner MFV *Atlantic Challenge,*
Executive Chairman Swan Net-Gundry Ltd.

ACKNOWLEDGEMENTS

My thanks to the following: Skipper Martin Howley, captain and co-owner of one of the most powerful trawlers afloat, for his foreword. My wife Ann, whose computer and patience I test in equal measure. My editor, Tony O'Callaghan. Trish O'Callaghan, whose perceptive critique of the early chapters helped shape the entire book. My son, Kevin Hayden, for his artwork and cover design. Seamus Magee, for his contribution in developing the initial design concept. My sponsors: Brendan Gill, skipper/owner of the 'Brendelen'; Eamonn McHugh, skipper/owner of the 'Antarctic'; John and Mary Hayden; Larry Murphy, skipper/owner of the 'Menhaden'; Michael Cavanagh, skipper/owner of the 'Fr. McKee'; Tony Byrne; skipper/owner of the 'Destiny'; Teddy O'Shea, skipper/owner of the 'Sheanne'; B. Hogan, skipper/owner of the 'Adrianne'; Neil Minihane, skipper/owner of the 'Sarah David; Walter Hay of Stuart Nets, Laurence Cavanagh of Cavanagh Nets; Ulster Bank Ltd, Killybegs; Tomas Conneely, skipper/owner of the 'Ocean Harvester'; Bord Iascaigh Mhara; Tommy Flaherty, skipper/owner of the 'Westward Isle'; Joseph Doherty, skipper/owner of the 'Aine', Liam and Margaret Hayden; Donal O'Neill, skipper/owner of the 'Dermot Anne'; skipper Laurie Irvine and the crew of the 'Antares; Coley Donohue, skipper/owner of 'Victory III'; Bill Lock and Brad Connally, skippers of the Alaskan vessels, 'Viking' and 'Westward I'; Martin Conneely, skipper/owner of 'Iuda Naofa'; James Enda Hayden and Rick Bakovic, alternate skippers and co-owners of 'F.V.Clyde'; Victor Buschini, skipper and co-owner of the 'Enterprise'; Katherine and Eric Black; Willie Williamson, skipper/owner of 'Research'; Mick O'Donnell, Island Seafoods; Alex Masson, skipper and co-owner of 'Kings Cross'; John McIntyre; John Peter Duncan, skipper, and his co-owners of 'Altaire'; James Kelly; Mrs Eileen Middleton; Peter and Julie Mullen of Irish Venture Inc.. Their sponsorship breathed life into the project; I am indebted to them.

CONTENTS

17 Seconds	1
Remembrance – 15 Years Later	8
April Fool	20
Just a Man	28
Contrition	37
Confession	42
Resolution	53
Revelation	61
The Third Day; Magic Numbers	68
Where Now?	71
Other Roads, Different Encounters	76
Close Your Eyes	81
The Question is Why?	86
It's Not Enough	91
Conaghan, OK; But What About Brennan?	99
Girls Night In / The Waiting	105
Recovered Memories, One	117
Recovered Memories, Two	126
Occluded Front	134
Mayday! Mayday!	143
Breaking News	154
The Diva ...	160
... And the Dance	172
Post-fatal Depression	185
All the Pretty Flowers	199
Final Entry	207

CHAPTER ONE

17 SECONDS

It was a sound like tearing canvas and it just didn't belong on the most powerful trawler afloat. I was in mid-step, foot already rising across the threshold of the wheelhouse door, and it spun me clean about. Francis Coll, the skipper, who was following me in off the command deck, had merely halted, and we stood there eyeball to eyeball. Each of us had one hand on the starboard rail, and the other on a handrail that tracked aft around the wheelhouse. We neither of us said anything, only listened. But in a habit born of childhood, I started counting. To myself.

One ---------

I don't know if I can adequately describe the scene to you. There was never a day like it. The sea was a liquid mirror stretching beyond even the circle of the horizon. The only thing was, there was no horizon. By some illusion of physics, some imperceptible vapour or unseen mist perhaps, the surface, silvered beyond anything I had ever seen, bled without an edge into the dome of the sky. The effect was of being centred on the base of an immense glass-bottomed bubble. A giant's plaything! Only the dark ridge of Slieve League away in the North-east, and Nephin and it's smaller twin in the South-east, betokened we were off Donegal Bay, on the deep edge. Nothing else showed. Not the Blue Stacks. Not the flat table of Ben Bulben. Not that most visible of mountains, Croagh Patrick. Nothing, Only our partner vessel, the year-old 'Great Adventure', and the older ship, 'Explorator', which was now operating as a research vessel.

Two ----------

Three ---------

Our ship was 'Ocean Voyager'. Scarcely six week's old, it was the most modern trawler in Europe, and at five thousand horsepower, was now the most powerful of her class in the world. Mind, this was - is - 1985.

Men who were there before us struggled to steal a living from the sea in the days of World War Two, in boats scarcely more than forty feet long, powered with old petrol-start Kelvin forty four horsepower engines. Their fuel ration was eleven gallons a month. Later, in the fifties, they advanced to seventy foot, one hundred and fifty two horsepower vessels, bought second hand out of Scotland, and pioneered at home in Ireland the new technique of mid-water trawling. By the end of the seventies, the new, hungry generation that grew at their knee had become the world masters of this technique, and by the eighties we had the 'Mackerel Millionaires' of Killybegs. Francis Coll was one of these. He was the most aggressive, the most daring, the most insatiable skipper of the lot. He was ruthless. He had taken eight hundred tons of fish in a single haul, and was ambitious to take a thousand. No. That's a lie. There was no limit to his ambition. The new vessel 'Ocean Voyager', of which he was the principal owner, with it's five thousand horsepower, was to be the means to that end. For the moment.

The trouble with this new super-powered vessel was that the nets, which Francis had specially constructed for him in Killybegs, were just too big physically to be modelled in any of Europe's test tanks. That's what had us out the bay on this particular morning. We were testing the newest of our pair-trawls: A monster with a gape bigger than Yankee Stadium. The 'Explorator', the research vessel which tracked along ahead of us, had streamed an under-water video camera astern and was even at this moment filming whatever was happening.

Fou -----------

Whoaaaaaaaaaaaa ---------------------

Without warning the ship heeled violently to starboard. Water shipped across the rail on the working deck aft. Our grip on the handrail about the wheelhouse was tested to the ultimate, and held. The tearing noise deepened, sharpened and rose in pitch, all in one, until it sounded like the diamond nails of a thousand banshees scraping the side of an obsidian mountain.

Five ---------

Six ---------

Then it ended. Equally violently, the vessel righted itself. The wall of water, which had shipped aboard the after deck, swept crew-men from starboard to port rail in an instant maelstrom. The shriek gone, the slap and slosh of a quarter of a million gallons of water clearing the scuppers was all that was heard. The supercharged snuffle of our five thousand turbo-driven horsepower and our partner's four and a half thousand, were as ever silent to us, so accustomed were we to this sound.

Seven ----------

The starboard trawl warp suddenly drew inboard. For an instant it kinked and looked like a sine curve, like a wave pattern on an oscilloscope. Then, as the sundered end of the cable cleared the surface astern and carried forward, whipping alongside the vessel at better than sixty miles an hour - maybe a hundred feet per second - realisation of what had really happened started to penetrate. Seven strand cable! Six by thirty six Warrington Seale with steel core. Two hundred and fifty two individual filaments of high carbon steel. The whole, laid up, thicker than a man's wrist. Eighty tons ultimate load. Torn apart atom from atom, it had heated to fifteen hundred degrees in the instant, and equally instantaneously had been tempered in the salt seawater of the North Atlantic. The end of each strand was a burnished rapier with a razor's edge.

Two seconds. What an eternity can pass through a man's mind in barely two seconds of time, and how hopelessly slow his reactions.

I once read that the crack of a whip - that sound that added so much drama to the equestrian acts that thrilled us when travelling circuses visited in our youth - is caused by the tip of the whip accelerating through the speed of sound in the final flip of the tightly plaited strands.

At my count of ten, two hundred and fifty two razors whipped in over the starboard rail and caught Francis Coll. His right upper arm was first to be hit but I never saw it. Then the lethal supersonic brush shredded a swathe three whole inches deep right through his torso and left arm, severing the entire upper portion of his body. Striking the deckhouse it tattooed a gunge of blood, bone, flesh and sinew millimetres deep into the very molecules of the metal. My arms, my hands, which I had been trying desperately to unlock from their handholds, finally moved, and virtually flew around his disconnected torso, and clutched it tight to me, chest to half-chest, virtually nose to nose.

That infernal, internal clock was still registering only ten.

Ten, and we were locked in this grotesque embrace of death. But Francis Coll wasn't dead. Yet. It was as if my breath needed to become his and I exhaled and exhaled and exhaled. Our faces were so close that it shouldn't have been possible for my eyes to focus on his face, but somehow they did. At thirteen he knew exactly what had happened to him. His mouth opened but no sound came. There was no breath to drive air over his vocal chords. His eyes spoke to me, but I don't know what they said. I had no interpreter.

Fifteen ----------

Sixteen ----------

Then eternity both ended and began.

At seventeen he was dead. My lungs sucked in as if they needed to draw the poison of pain out of the deepest wound in the whole world.

Ehhhhhhhhh-h-h-h-h-------------

It was as if I still drew breath for both of us, sucking in all the regenerative oxygen, the very ozone itself of this immense ocean. Then it reversed and the scream came.

Aaahaahhhhh-h-h-h-h---------- ------ -------

The voice-activated intercom picked it up and relayed it on all the decks of the 'Ocean Voyager'. In the wheelhouse, the open band on the radio picked it up, and the intercoms of the 'Great Adventure' and the 'Explorator' in turn, and it echoed back to me from each of them, out of synch.

We were delayed overnight once, in Oslo, as we travelled to the yard in which the vessel was built in Alesund, and I visited the National Gallery. I have seen Edvard Munch's painting 'The Scream'. On this morning I became it.

It was ten minutes before the spasm in the two severed hands relaxed sufficiently for the fingers to unlock and the unconnected limbs fell to the deck. By that time I had over-toppled with the weight of Francis Coll's half-torso and fell across his lower body which had slumped forward.

That is how the crew found us. It was at least another fifteen minutes before they succeeded in prising my grip loose from the partial corpse of what had so recently been a man. Crewmen on the other vessels that thought to snap photographs as they came alongside ran retching for the rail when they realised what they were actually focusing on. It was another hour before I discovered that shards of the wire had shredded my own body-warmer and the shirt beneath it, and had sliced tramlines across my chest.

In that confusion, it was no wonder little heed was paid to the submarine that breached about half a mile off, like some enormous unmarked black whale, and sounded almost as quickly as it had appeared.

This is no lie. That's how it happened. Don't ask me the day or the date. I don't ever want to hear the day or the date, ever again. It wasn't only Francis Coll that died that day. I met Death that morning and looked him square in the eye, then walked on from him. But he has already taken my soul, and he knows me for who I am. Let you know also. I am Owen Friel, and I will have payment, even if it takes me to the very day I die. I won't discount the bill even for death itself.

CHAPTER TWO

REMBRANCE - 15 YEARS LATER

I have always believed that just such a tape existed. The event, the horrific accident it described, was so bizarre that somebody was bound to have recorded it. But this was the first time I had verification – of the existence of a tape, not of the event. The event will live with me forever. It was too horribly real, too close to me, to ever forget. How many is it given to, to know so graphically how their father died? Francis Coll was my father.

"How did Conaghan have such a tape?"

That's the question I asked myself as soon as my brain cleared enough to think,

"and not to have shared the secret until now."

My father died fifteen years ago. I was only seven then. Seven years, five months, sixteen days.

I put the question to Conaghan:

"How come you have such a tape?" I asked, "and never let on until now?"

He just looked at me.

"There are some things….. It wasn't the whole…… It just didn't feel right. The greatest scoop I ever had, and I didn't use it."

"Why now, then?" I asked him. He dodged the question.

"Did you recognise the voice?" he asked.

"Instantly."

That was the truth. Almost on the first syllable. He was such a part of my growing up.

"Owen Friel", I answered.

"Yes" he said, "Owen Friel. He's for early release, you know."

I didn't know and it took a turn out of me.

"When?" said I.

Again he dodged the question.

"Could you cover the release? Would you be up to it?"

Now it was my turn to dodge. Conaghan was the editor, the man who had hired me. Instead of asking back "Am I up for it?" I responded by asking did he know who I was.

"Of course" he answered, "Ruan O'Colla is not much of a disguise for Ruan Coll. You are Francis Coll's son; and Frances' son.

I flinched at the mention of my mother. It was almost not fair to call her by her name; she had been murdered.

"When?   How long?"

I didn't need to finish either question; he was there ahead of me.

"From the first day you asked for a job on the paper. Any job. Even before. I was a staff reporter when the accident happened, and covered the story and the funeral. And the...   Your mother...   When she disappeared. The paper was just the 'The Correspondent' then. That was before we went national."

I made no other response.

"Soon" he continued, "real soon. That's the answer to your question, but before you decide, listen to this second tape." Then he pressed the eject button, removed the tape he had just played and took a second cassette from a drawer in his desk.

"This came in the mail just two days ago. Just it; not a note, not even a scrap of paper with it. Just a fragment of bubblewrap. Even the postmark is anonymous. One of those Post Office franking machines. Only a code number. Not that that's a problem."

He loaded it, then hesitated.

"Play it" I said. "Whatever it is, play it."

I was slow; I didn't recognise the voice. Not at first. There was too much stress in it.

" **Fuck you. What more do you want? God you want everything. You want to know every fucking thing. Don't you know only God knows everything and he doesn't tell the likes of us? He keeps us in the dark. In the fucking dark, do you hear, and lets us find out for ourselves. Why don't you do that? Find out for your self. You're the fucking detective. Ha ha ha ha ha ! That's it. You're the fucking detective. You find out. Ha ha ha ha."**

Then it hit me. Of course it was! Owen Friel, but not as I had ever known him: The voice more than angry. I stopped the tape, rewound it, and played that first bit again. Yes. It was him. Then there was a pause, a small bit of a break. Something wiped from the tape, perhaps. Then a sound again.

"UH!   U-u-u-h."

As if he was hit; or fell.

"What did you do that for? You'd no call to do that. Haven't I told you everything I know? That's the truth. I was brought up to tell the truth. I don't lie. But if it's memory you want, I'll tell you about memory. You don't know what memory is. The curse of the Irish; that's what it is. We forget nothing. We remember everything. Don't you know that?

He paused; to take a breath, maybe. Then the voice started again, the words spewing out of him.

We have folk memories of trees, giants that stood before the pyramids were built, but people call it myth. They're the clever ones.

When Christ was being crucified, a priest, a blind druid, a shaman of the old religion, saw – saw, I tell you – saw it happening, and took an axe to the old god, the crooked one; Crom, the sun god of the Celts. He felled the idol, more than four hundred years before Patrick did the same at Darragh Fort, and I can still show you where it stood. I can dig out the hole for you. I did it once. An old man showed me and I only a boy. How's that for memory for you?"

He continued at a rush.

"It's like these bruises on my ribs. I'll remember them. Every one of them. I'll finger them like a musician fingers the holes on a tin whistle, and I'll carry the tune with me to the grave. But I'll play it over your grave first. Never forget that, O'Hara. I'll play it in jig-time, and dance to it. You remember that one. Hit me again if you want to, but be warned, you will

```
only add to the tune. Give me a breather and I'll
tell you what more I know. But I can't tell you
what I don't know. And I don't know if what's
driving you is jealousy. So many were jealous of
our success. What cause had they to be? We were
just getting our turn on top of the wheel."
```

He paused, sorting out the jigsaw of his own thoughts, perhaps.

```
"Where to start? That's the question."
```

```
"Mary Katherine. It has to be Mary Katherine."
```

But really it started long before that. I grew up with this and knew what was coming

Our grandfathers, or their grandfathers; or other ancestors farther back again; were the ones left behind when Red Hugh, the 'O'Donnell', fled with the other Earls to Spain. They had defied Elizabeth, and had stood against her man, Bingham, when he thought to march around the shore to ambush Grace O'Malley as she attacked Killybegs. Abandoned, they made a refuge on the slopes of the Blue Stack Mountains in Donegal. It was as if the sea had been a hundred fathoms deeper, and they just to have made their settlement as they stepped ashore. From this wilderness they defied even nature itself. They survived the snows that buried Ireland when the Thames froze. They endured Cromwell and William of Orange, and survived both of them and a famine. Hurricanes, that seeded themselves in steamy equatorial waters, and used the Caribbean islands as a space rocket might use one of the outer planets for a sling-shot effect, were caught in the 'catcher's mitt' of Donegal Bay where they exhausted themselves against the stone walls of their white-washed cabins. Maybe their culture didn't survive; not the way it was, only the memory of it. But their language did. Only just. Gaelic: The third language written in Europe after Greek and Latin. 'Irish' to you and me: To me in any case. But in our townland it almost died at our parent's generation. That it did not was down to an outsider, an Island-woman, who married into the place. Mary Katherine! Mary Katherine, who married Stephen Coll, my grandfather on my mother's side!

This was what I heard Owen Friel tell some anonymous interrogator on the tape, and then:

"You wouldn't know any of that. You're not one of us. You don't belong, here or anywhere. What are you? A fucking cop. Pardon my French. A flic."

There was another, longer pause. Something else wiped. I opened my mouth to say something, then stopped as Conaghan raised a finger. The voice, when it resumed, had an extra catch in it. Not an emotional catch, more a physical one, as if the person speaking had cracked a rib, and couldn't breathe easily. And it was the more noticeable for his trying to sing. A bit of doggerel: No recognisable tune.

"All the birds of the air were a-sighing and a-sobbing"

"Who killed him? That's what you want to know, isn't it? Who killed fucking Cock Robin? Only it wasn't Cock Robin, was it? It was the Fly."

Again a bit of a pause, then

"You know nothing. You don't know about the Fly. 'I, said the fly, I saw him die.' Only he didn't, because it was he that died, and even if he did see, he can't tell us."

I knew then where he was coming from, but not yet where he was going. All to do with family and friendships, bonds formed in childhood; and with Mary Katherine. Mary Katherine who, when my mother disappeared, died, if die she did, was both Grandmother and Mother to me, as well as teacher.

I didn't hear the tape anymore with thinking of them.

There were two families of Coll's in our townland; Frank's and Stephen's, neither related to the other, and a whole bunch of Slevin's, Brogan's and Breslin's; Friel's too of course, and Brennans. Frank was, unsurprisingly, my father's father. Stephen and his wife, Mary Katherine, were my mother's parents. They had only two children: Twin girls, Frances Maria and Martina. Frances Maria was my mother.

Stephen and Mary Katherine, both of whom were at the time in their late twenties, met and married in New York, and against the run of the times moved back to the depression that scattered so many out of Ireland in the fifties. That was after Stephen's father died.

Mary Katherine came from a different place. Born an islander and a native Irish speaker, she qualified as a teacher, then emigrated, first to England, then on the post-war £10 assisted passage scheme to Australia. Two years later she moved again, to the United States, and landed in California. She didn't stop however, and continued on to New York. There she became an actress, an exotic kind of a creature flitting in and out of the dream time world of Greenwich Village. It was there she met this other Irish émigré, Stephen, who succeeded in getting to America by signing on to fight in the Korean War, then fell back into construction work about New York. Reared on folk memories of hedge-schools taught by travelling scholars fluent in Latin and Greek, as well as their native Gaelic, he too drifted about the 'Village'; searching without knowing what it was he was searching for. That was until he met Mary Katherine.

It was Stephen himself who told this to me, after my parents died.

Two whole trunks of books she took with her into the Blue Stacks, and allowed no rest, no peace to her newly acquired husband until he had torn apart and rebuilt the family home to her satisfaction. It seemed at first that she sacrificed everything that was traditional about the cottage. But when the new structure took shape it still retained the protection of two foot thick stone walls, and preserved at the back of an enlarged living area the traditional Donegal 'outshot' – an alcove just big enough to take a curtained-off marriage bed. All this, my grandfather told me. But she added depth and width to the hearth to create a 'cluid', a traditional thing in her own native place. With room for both a crib and a rocking chair, it protected both the beginning and the end of life. An extra room, a library, a social area, was added, and an extra bedroom. They expected children. But the children, when they came, were two only; twin girls. And the big room with it's distinctive panorama of windows that captured, in the distance, her beloved ocean, became in turn nursery, kindergarten, classroom, and, when other children were invited in – theatre.

At the time the house was built, it must have seemed a castle.

Mary Katherine came to rule another classroom also. When one of the two teachers in the local school died, she applied for the position and was astute enough to show the necessary deference to get the job. That secured, she immediately set about subverting the whole legacy of deference that stifled Irish society at the time. It was as if she had enlarged her family of two girls to encompass the children of more than twenty families spread across no less than five townlands. They were the first in perhaps a dozen generations to be reared with hope, and she opened her mind and her house to them.

"You can be a ring of gold" she told them, "through your bonds with one another, and that will become the first link in a golden chain that will stretch out to the next generation, and the next, and the next again."

She told us as much, a generation later.

She taught them to distinguish the genuine from false gold by standing them in the storm-moon's light and quoting -- "Last night the moon had a golden ring and tonight no moon I see", had them measure the days until the storm broke. The Sun, she insisted, like the ancient Egyptians and the pre-Celts before her, was a fire of gold, and she bid them rise to it in the morning and track westwards in it's wake to discover their own fortune in life. For most of them, that westwards was to the growing port of Killybegs and the silver harvest in the ocean beyond. Some went even further, and skippered vessels that fished the far Pacific and the edges of the Arctic ice.

It was as if Owen Friel and I were both reading from the same rehearsed script, and I suddenly was aware that his cracked voice was echoing mine. I was back in Conaghan's office again, and Conaghan was looking at me.

"It's amazing the baggage we carry with us from our childhood" I said to him, "even nursery rhymes. She taught us everything."

Then I let the tape run on, uninterrupted. Owen Friel was on a roll, seemingly oblivious to any interrogation. saying just what it pleased him-self to say.

"Some of us she seemed drawn to more than others - myself and Anthony Killoge, for instance. When Anthony and I talked between ourselves about it at the time, we put it down to the fact that both our mothers had died; mine in giving birth to me; Anthony's shortly after he was born; and we let it go at that. You should mark that; how close we were."

He mentioned my father's name then, and the friendship that was more than a friendship that developed between them even when they were children.

"Maybe we were jealous; they had something that we hadn't. Maybe that was it, and we called 'Franciss Francess' after them. When we did that, Mary Katherine merely turned away to hide her smile, but she had her own sharpness and her own way of showing it."

I couldn't believe what he was doing. He was being interrogated by some bastard who was knocking hell out of him; and here he was, he was reliving his childhood, and admitting to jealousy of one of the two people he was accused of murdering.

" One day she caught Anthony Killoge chanting it - we were aged only six or seven I suppose - and she staged a little dramatisation in the classroom of 'Who killed Cock Robin?', casting Anthony as the 'Fly'. We all knew that Anthony's surname translated literally as 'fly', and so he became forever and for all of us 'The Fly'. My own punishment for chanting this name after him maybe five years later was to stand atop a nearby crag in a rising gale and shout aloud a passage she gave me to read:

'Spit rain. Spout fire. I tax you not you elements with unkindness.'

I shouted it. I can remember it still. I never called Anthony 'Fly' ever again."

I looked at Conaghan in disbelief. "What was he thinking of?" I asked him. He just shrugged. I let the tape run on and made no more interruptions.

"When Francis Coll and I, and some half a dozen of the others, went to sea, Anthony Killoge got himself apprenticed to an Electronics company over by Killybegs. And when Francis and I took the 'Ocean Voyager' on that ill-fated trial that morning, Anthony Killoge was the technician in charge of the underwater filming aboard the 'Explorator'. And when I stumbled ashore that evening in Killybegs, still drenched in the blood of Francis Coll, it was Anthony Killoge who thrust a video cassette into my hand and said: "Keep that. You will want it". And when I called to Anthony's house the morning of Francis' funeral, it was not Anthony who answered the door. In fact no one did. And when I let myself in and searched the house, I discovered why he didn't let me in. He couldn't. He was dead. He was stuffed, naked, into the bath, a plastic bag drawn down tightly over his head and knotted. His eyes were open."

It was only then I realised where he was getting to; and why he seemed so controlled in the telling. He was reliving everything. When he said: "Who saw him die?" I mouthed it involuntarily myself. When he said he screamed an awfully long time, I knew just exactly how long he screamed; and when he said he then went outside and puked all over the grass, it was as much as I could do not to throw up all over Conaghan's desk. And still the narrative continued.

"Our golden circle was coming apart. Francis Coll's death had broken the link, but it was an accident. This death was different. Anthony Killoge was murdered. I tore the plastic bag off his face, because it offended me to think of the obscene way in which his death had come about; and I compressed his chest, with his mouth and nose under the water, so that some of the bath-water might go into the lungs, and make it seem as if he drowned in his sleep. I knew it to happen once before. A girl that I knew! Then, I drove off to the funeral. As I neared the town, I wound down the window of the car and threw out the plastic bag and watched it in the rear view mirror as it blew away into the ditch to join all the other rubbish."

"Surely that was it," I thought. The tape was almost at an end, and there was a break as if something else had been erased, or patched in.

"That's it. I'm telling you no more. You know who killed him better than I do. Find him, or them. There had to be more than one of them. Common sense would tell you. You should know that. You're the fucking detective."

"Gotcha!"

That, finally, was the end; the last voice someone else's.

"Who?" I asked.

"O'Hara. He was a detective."

"Was?" I asked.

"Was," said Conaghan, "He died two years ago."

"Owen Friel can dance on his grave then," I said, bitterly.

"Maybe I'll get Doyle to cover the release," said Conaghan, "he's reliable."

"Don't you f—" The words rose in my mouth, and I choked them off.

"No," I said, "it's mine."

"It's not a promise", said Conaghan.

CHAPTER THREE

APRIL FOOL

"What they have done is simply brilliant."

That's what I told Jenny Stronnach. She's my photographer. On this assignment. She didn't seem at all impressed. Not by her response at any rate.

"What are you on about?" she asked.

"The Prison!" I answered.

"More accurately, the Prison Authorities. They have succeeded in hiding an entire prison. Not just any jail, but Portlaoise Prison for god's sake. The highest security prison in the State. You would think it no more than a factory."

Maybe that's what prisons are: Factories. The murderers, muggers, rapists and petty thieves are only the raw material. We are aware of them as such, just as we are aware of trainloads of ore being delivered to a smelter, or of 'chips' being bulk-delivered to a plastic extrusion plant. We know little of the processes involved and, apart from a general kind of a curiosity, we don't want to know. We're happy only to see a finished product, all shaped and shiny. A stainless steel cooking pot. A plastic drip tray for the dishwasher. A reformed, anonymous ex-prisoner. One we don't have to worry about any more.

Stronnach still didn't seem impressed. But then I hadn't put these thoughts together yet. That came later. This was that day in Conaghan's office he gave us the assignment. I already told you he was the editor. Mind you, I lobbied him for weeks to get it. Getting Stronnach was a bonus I didn't expect. She's the best photographer on the paper. Maybe Conaghan wanted more from this story than I thought he did.

We went for a pint afterwards, Stronnach and I, to the Palace Bar. It's still old-fashioned. Painted wood-panelled snugs and a mahogany bar. There's always a private corner. I filled her in on Owen Friel. What I knew of him, and what I didn't know. He was jailed for one murder, suspected of an implication in several others. He admitted nothing and by instruction to his solicitor presented no defence. It caused consternation in court and riots outside. There were many for him, others totally against. His alleged victims were Anthony Killoge and a woman, Frances Coll. Her body was never found. That's just what I told Jenny Stronnach. I stumbled verbally in the telling. She looked at me. I could feel it. But I kept looking past her to the scrap of a mirror behind the bar. Eventually her eyes caught mine and I opened my mouth to continue. I turned to look at her.

"Did anyone ever tell you how attractive you are?" I asked her.

She just thumped me on the arm.

She was attractive. No. More than attractive: There was a magnetism, an aphrodisiac quality, about her. I paused yet again.

It was Jenny Stronnach who spoke next. She moved the conversation forward.

"What about the conviction?" she asked.

"Twenty years," I said. "Mandatory life. The police case prevailed." And I went on to tell her just how slight that case was.

It was based on the police account of what he garbled when he stumbled into a County Donegal police station over fifteen years ago, and on flecks of blood that were discovered on the clothes he was wearing. I don't know how they established it was her blood, because they never discovered her body.

"How come you know so much about it?" she asked, and looked at me yet again.

"No wonder she's such a good photographer" I thought, "She can see the soul."

"Because she was my mother" I answered her. "Frances Coll was my mother", and the emphasis was on the "my".

"Jesus!" she said.

"Do you not wish him dead", she questioned me; "I would." But I made no answer.

"Jesus," she said yet again, "What an assignment!"

I remembered Conaghan trying to tell another reporter how good Jenny Stronnach was.

"You only describe it;" he said. "She makes you see it."

Then the final accolade.

"Things happen around her."

Now I could see it. She was a cosmic version of the vinegar I was told old engineers used to free rust-locked screw threads. Five minutes and a pint and she had unwound my own lock-nut. As easily as if it were lubricated with some super-silicone. Half my secret gone. Mentally I screwed the stopper back again. I ran a diversion. I played the two tapes for her. The tape that Conaghan had kept under wraps all those years, and the tape that had been posted anonymously.

While she listened I straightened back on the stool, the better to look at her, then bent my head to the one half of the headset we were sharing. A paradox! We had privacy in that most public of places. One either side of a narrow shelf of a fixed table in one of the snugs. A high shelf! Tall stools. Room only to lay elbow to wrist of one forearm along the edge of the shelf. Heads and shoulders thrown forward towards each other. We breathed each other's exhaled breath. Our noses were at risk each time the other lifted a glass. We were so close that each looked down. To have faced each other would have involved an eye contact too immediate to bear. That's why I sat back. A defensive move. I was the one who yielded.

She looked up. Eyes as grey as hazel bark looked searchingly at me. She turned her head away briefly. When she looked again, the pupils were as freshly green as the hazel leaves in May. Some trick of the light.

"How old is she?" I thought, "Twenty six, maybe. No. More. Thirty one, thirty two-ish. Ten years the better of me." A neat nose, and blonde hair. Well, pale ginger. Not too long, it was lightly frizzed. It suited her.

"Well" she said, "Do I pass?"

I flustered. She let it go.

"Tell me about the prison" she said.

That was easy. Easier still to show her. We travelled the afternoon before, and pulled up onto the path across from the prison. It was broad and clearly used by others for parking also. Just at the entrance to a Council yard. The two pseudo-bungalows that screened the original cut-stone gatehouse were not quite directly opposite us, but it was clear how effective they were at disguising the prison entrance. The strong pyracantha hedge, backing the ordinary looking suburban-style wall and iron fencing, added to the camouflage, so that even the new guard-block with the weld-mesh screening didn't impinge on the eye. Further out the old Dublin road an extensive parking area, set within the fence, backed onto a new-looking seamless concrete wall that looked to be about twenty feet high. This was topped with a broad concrete beading that clearly would allow no purchase for any kind of grappling iron. But all in all, it looked just like any other provincial factory in any other provincial town.

We left it at that till the morning.

We were late in the morning, later than I had wanted to be. It was gone a quarter past five when we pulled onto the path again, the windows of the car still white with frost. I had wanted to be there for five. A faulty alarm clock in the B&B, and the man's insistence on making us at least a pot of tea, delayed us. "Keep the engine running," said Jenny, "I need the cameras warm. If they get cold, my breath could fog the lenses." And we waited.

An hour and a half we waited, and my blood pulsed like an alarm that could not be switched off. Everything told me that Owen Friel would want an early morning release, and it was already on the turn for seven. A lone figure emerged from the entrance. One of the guards, seemingly. Whoever it was, was dressed in prison uniform. He crossed the road in our direction, and started scraping frost off the windscreen of a car that was parked nearby. I stepped out of the 'Espace' I had borrowed for comfort's sake, without saying what I wanted it for. I asked him if he could help us.

"Was Owen Friel released this morning?" I asked.

He looked at me a moment before answering. "Yes he said. "He was. More than two hours ago."

"F—k!" I said. I couldn't help but say it.

I could see a cartoon image of myself growing jackass ears. In another image a glowing neon-sign flashed "April Fool".

The date was April the first. April 1st, 2000; What a gobshite!

"What road do you think he would have taken?" This was Stronnach's voice, more polite than I had ever heard her. And the funny thing was, she got a very helpful answer.

"I think he has gone straight for Donegal. He has talked about nowhere else since this possibility came up. I'm sure he would have taken the Tullamore road."

And only just delaying to ask best directions, and to garble our thanks, we took off for town first, then at maximum speed out the Tullamore Road. All fingers crossed.

Clearing the town and with a long straight ahead of us I shoed the accelerator. We built up a head of speed, then, on the first bend, I nearly lost it on an icy patch. Chastened, I eased back somewhat. Bad enough to have to face Conaghan without a story: Worse to have to face Mary Katherine with a wrecked Espace. It was her car.

"Take it easy, won't you?"

This was Stronnach, who was stretched across the car behind me, her bum on one seat, her arm about her cameras on another. When we were parked across from the prison she had tried to tell me what cameras and lenses she was using, and what film. 3200 ISO colour film in her best camera, a Minolta Dynax 700 SI, she said, with a 70 to 210mm lens. To be able to zoom in on the prison entrance, she continued, in the early morning darkness. I heard the detail without really taking it in. She had a second camera also with a less powerful zoom. An old 'Canon' I think she said, loaded with 1600 speed film; and, yet another "ordinary" camera.

"Go easy, for Christ's sake" she said again, "If he's on the road, we'll catch up with him."

I suppose that was it, really. I couldn't bring myself to believe he was on the road.

I watched the miles on the clock. Five miles, six miles gone. Eight miles! The sun was rising directly behind, and cast the long shadow of the car down the straight in front of us. The hedges on either side were white with a heavy hoar-frost. Even the briars were picked out. A bank of tall dark Beech trees screened off the fields on the right hand side of the road. I slowed, more in doubt than on account of a kink of an S-bend. Beyond it, I straightened the car up again. A lone figure swinging a bag was striding out before us. I had no doubt any more. Owen Friel!

"Drive on past him, until I tell you to stop."

This was Jenny Stronnach again.

"And when you get out of the car, walk back to meet him. But open the back door of the car before you do so. This has got a back door, hasn't it? If it opens upwards, it can act as a lens hood."

I made her no answer but pulled up when she said so, and opened up the back door of the 'Espace' as she requested, and walked back along the road towards that other lone walking figure. But this wasn't for her. This was for me.

This was one of those mornings you needed to be up and about yourself to really experience. Others could describe it to you, or even write about it, but you needed to be there to know the wholeness of it. Air that carried the very frost into your lungs. A glistening whiteness on the earth, as if it were the soul of the first man that stood and walked upon it. A red sun that could have been thirty or three hundred feet across. Still screened by that black bank of beech trees, I lifted my hand high to shade my eyes from the high brightness. He lifted his hand maybe to do the same. I called his name.

"Owen" I said, "Owen Friel."

Recognition came very slowly to him. Chemical messengers scanned forgotten pathways in his brain. Neurotransmitters faltered in their response. It was three quarters of a decade since he last saw me, that one occasion that I visited him in prison. The time I decided to find out for myself. His hand was a defensive shield.

"Ruan" he answered. "Is it Ruan Coll?"

I guess that's when she snapped us, dark against the dark of the trees. When I saw the prints afterwards, I couldn't believe the resolution she had achieved: The collar, folds and creases in the back of my jacket were clearly visible, to say nothing of my ears and the back of my neck. The back of my raised hand was white against the black of the trees, which offset perfectly the prison pallor in the face of Owen Friel. His hand was a silhouette against the brightness of the sky. When we got back to the car, I introduced him to Jenny Stronnach.

"Meet Owen Friel," I said. "He's my Godfather!"

"Jesus God!" she exclaimed.

"I think not" he answered her. "Just a man."

A fragment, a couple of words, from some lesson of Mary Katherine's, flashed across my memory. I breathed it softly.

"Ecce Homo."

CHAPTER FOUR

JUST A MAN

Diary entry, April 1st, 2000
Jenny Stronnach's journal.

He was just a man. I don't know what else I could have expected. Not quite a six-footer; a metre eighty, I'd say. Mid forties. Had, still has, a good head of dark hair. What am I writing? Past tense, present tense. I only met him today for chrissake. What a bloody day! Where did this come from? What have I got into? He looks older than mid-forties, though. It's that pallor. Like an old lady's, an old lady that hasn't left the house in years. Almost translucent. I'd like to photograph him, before he loses it, but where do I find him?

We were lucky this morning, both to find him and in where we found him. Lucky to have such a combination of film and lenses. I'm still not sure what I snapped. It was just one of those encounters that make the hair at the back of the neck prickle, and the pictures capture it. The other pictures captured it also, but they weren't right for the story. Not this part of it in any case. And they involve Ruan. I'll save them. For later.

I can't believe how silent he was. We drove all the way from the Clara road – it was really on the Clara road that we met him – all the way through Clara, then on to Tullamore and round the ring road, then as far as the Galway – Dublin road, heading west, and he never said a word. Only raised his hand in a 'no' when I took up the small camera to photograph him in the car. He just sat there all the time, drinking in the passing scene. Ruan tried his best to draw him into conversation, but without success. I felt sorry for Ruan. This was both personal and a story, and I don't think he would have attempted it without backup. I could be wrong, though. A youngster, who lost both his parents in the way he did, and has survived at all, has to have something special going for him.

He startled both of us; Owen Friel did; put the heart crossways in both of us with the suddenness of the shout.

"STOP."

We were crossing the Shannon over the new bridge on the Athlone bypass.

Funny how the hum of tyres on smooth tarmac can lull a body. Then again, it was warm in the cocoon of the Espace. Warm inside, and cold without!

The river was high; swollen with snow-melt.

It had been a hard winter. Shannon Pot, the source of the river, fully sixty miles away in the border-mountains of Cavan and Leitrim, had all but frozen over in January. In February I was on assignment, photographing deer as they foraged in the snow along the shores of Lough Allen. The lake itself, all of sixteen hundred feet lower than Shannon Pot, is the navigable headwater of the river.

It snowed again only a week since – I caught the images on the late TV evening news. Ridiculously, even this late in the year, April 1st, Slieve an Iarainn and Cuilcagh, two of the mountains that ring Lough Allen, wore glistening white caps. I could see them gleaming in the sunshine far to the north.

"Ridiculous!" I thought, and looked again at the dark, swollen water of the river. A breath of an east wind sent shivers across the surface.

"STOP!" he shouted again. "BACK UP!"

There was little else Ruan could do except what he said, and the car had scarcely stopped, when Owen was out of it, carrying his grip-bag, ran back to the east side of the bridge, vaulted the safety barrier, and ran down the bank to the river's edge. We scrambled after him to the rail, and were only in time to see him swing the grip-bag high into the air and release it at the top of the swing. It soared out towards mid river. I cursed myself for being caught unawares and ran for the car. I grabbed the first camera that came to hand. Too late, I thought of the high-speed film and stopped the lens down as far as it could go. A thousandth of a second would have to do. I ran for the rail again.

Nothing could have prepared me for what next I saw. A birth-naked Owen Friel was up to his thighs in the Shannon. The bank behind him gleamed with the white hoar. His arm, stretched back behind him, holding what I took to be his clothes, started to sweep forward. I hit the motorised exposure button and pointed the camera almost aimlessly. I was myself on auto-focus. His prison-issue clothes flew over the water. The surface was black, like a lacquered mirror, and reflected perfectly every flutter of the shirt and vest and underpants as they floated down into the stream. Then he plunged out into the river, almost as if he intended to retrieve them.

"Jesus Christ."

"What the fuck."

I don't think I had ever heard Ruan Coll – easier on the tongue than O'Colla, I must admit – use such language. More like my own. I certainly never heard such alarm in his voice.

He had already vaulted the barrier himself, and was down on the bank of the river, gesticulating at Owen Friel who by that time was being swept steadily downstream. Ruan hesitated only a moment, then stripped hurriedly to vest and underpants and dived into the ice-fringed water. I snapped away until the dull click betokened I was out of film and had half started back to the car for one of the other cameras when the reality hit me. These two could drown! I climbed the barrier myself and ran down the bank on a diagonal to catch up to them.

I hurdled a fence, then almost tripped on a branch, a willow or something like it, quite light really, and I picked it up and reached it out towards them. Ruan had hold of Owen, and was struggling to draw him to the shore. The branch I was holding didn't quite reach far enough and I waded out up to my waist. Jesus but it was cold. Ruan grabbed the branch with his one free hand and I backed in towards the bank, struggling for footing, holding on grimly to the butt of the branch with both hands. Finally, I made it to the edge and collapsed backwards onto my own butt, and Ruan got his footing and was able to transfer his second hand to Owen Friel.

A torrent of words flowed out of him. I don't think I ever heard such verbal abuse, certainly never such bad language. Suddenly the two of them were on the bank again and it was over, almost as quickly as it began. But the adrenaline explosion from Ruan continued in full eruption.

"Never do anything like fucking that again. What the fuck do you think you're playing at? Trying to fucking drown all of us? You're not getting fucking off that fucking easy."

Then the two men collapsed in each other's arms and sobbed. I had to shout at them to get dressed. Well at Ruan. The other man just stood there, still as naked as the day he was born. The pallor had now turned a deathly blue, every muscle shivering. Hypothermia was setting in. I picked up the camera from where I had left it down and climbed the bank back again to the car. Careless of the passing traffic I stripped off my own wet things and pulled on dry pants and jeans. Then I searched Ruan's bag and finding no real change of clothes threw down a jumper that I found and a coat.

"Better get Owen into these, and get him up here into the car." I shouted. Then I climbed back into the car myself and turned up the heat. The engine was still running.

I don't know if it was the shock of what had nearly happened, or the effect of my own immersion in the river, but I found myself unable to speak. When I tried to, I couldn't get a comprehensible word out without chattering. Ruan was the opposite. It was almost as if he had been recharged. He bundled Owen Friel unceremoniously into the front passenger seat, slammed the door shut, and climbed in the driver's door.

"The Lakeside Hotel. That's where we'll go. I know them there. We need to get him into a warm bed. It's only five minutes away." And he gunned the 'Espace' out into the traffic, heedless, totally, of what cars were coming.

He certainly did know them at the hotel, and they him, because there was no hesitation, no delay, and a minimum of fuss in getting us accommodated in the double-bedded room he had requested. Pausing at the door only long enough to order hot chocolate, and a couple of hot-water bottles, he wasted no time in stripping Owen Friel of the coat and jumper and man-handling him into the bed.

"Strip off" he shouted at me, "Quick. Down to your bra and pants. Look lively. We've no time for modesty."

He, himself, was already in the process of discarding his shirt jacket and trousers. He just dropped them on the floor. I guess his vest and underpants must have been discarded on the bank of the river.

"In, into the bed" he shouted again. "You can cuddle up to his backside. I'll lie at his front."

Only then did he explain what he was doing. Standard procedure for seamen hauled out of freezing water. The most effective way of warming them. Weird. Weird and cold. I don't think I was ever as cold. The three of us shivered together uncontrollably. And in no way co-ordinated.

A knock at the door! I don't know what the room-service waiter thought, for he got and was offered no explanation when Ruan's hand just took the hot water bottles from him, and the tray of cups and jug of chocolate, with the reach of a hand around the half-opened door. Then he closed it again. It surprised me that he even said thanks, but he did. The only thing that he said. Then he wrapped the hot water bottles in towels, threw them into the bed, and climbed back in himself.

Unbelievably, I fell asleep. Waking, I didn't know at first either where I was, or what I was doing. Ruan had just got out of bed and was pulling on his trousers. He paused when he saw the unasked question in my eyes, and mouthed "About an hour." My eyes scanned his body from head to thighs. He wasn't at all bad looking and I liked what I saw. Suddenly he realised that he was wearing no underpants and he turned his back on me while he finished pulling on his trousers, adjusted himself, and fastened the zip. I started to laugh.

"It's a bit late to think of modesty," I said, "or worry about nudity."

Then it struck me.

"God, he's still a virgin!" I thought, and I laughed some more, but differently.

He shushed me to silence and said: "Don't wake him."

I had almost forgotten the other man in the bed. The torpor that was on him was gone, and he appeared now to be in a sound sleep. He still trembled, though, from time to time in a faint shiver. Ruan poured himself a cup of chocolate from the flask left by the room-service waiter, and sat half sideways on the edge of the bed drinking it. It appeared to be still warm.

"I'm going into town to get some clothes for him. And for myself." He said quietly. "I expect I'll be the guts of an hour."

I could see that both men were about the same height, but I thought that Owen Friel was thicker about the chest and waist. I said so.

"And in the neck. Get a size or two bigger in the shirt collar. And get him a jumper, a wool one, not synthetic." I knew. I have brothers. Then a parting shot:

"Don't forget the underpants. For yourself." And I laughed again.

Blushing, he retreated out the door and hung the 'Do not disturb' notice on the door-handle outside. Then he was gone.

I was on my own - IN BED - with Owen Friel.

When Ruan was in the bed, my free arm rested across both men, my hand just lying lightly on Ruan's arm. Now my arm bent easily at the elbow and my hand lay on Owen Friel's chest. It was a muscular chest, more so than I had expected. Hadn't he just spent fourteen or fifteen years in prison? I don't know what started working in my brain, then, but that visual curiosity that is at the root of my own vocation compelled me to explore. My hand moved from the 'pecs' to the 'abs'. I sensed the same thing in both: An extraordinary level of fitness. I tried consciously to let my hand just glide over his skin. The way a blind person might feel your face, I thought; not really touching, more a sensory thing. As if my palm was a receptor for positively charged electrons discharging themselves continuously from his epidermis. Below his navel I felt the first tickle of body hair. Bold now, I let my hand glide on downwards. Without actually feeling it, I knew my hand was just over his penis.

I never felt him move. Suddenly, my hand was overlaid with his bigger palm. Startled, my hand curled in reaction, and I found myself holding his penis, and his hand was like a living lock on mine. We just lay there. I felt my embarrassment colour me to my toes, and my skin burned with heat. Five minutes, at least, we lay there. His penis hardened into an erection. Then equally suddenly, his two hands swung me round, and I found myself on my back with him kneeling over me. His hands moved up under my breasts.

"Take off your bra," he instructed me, and he lifted up the arch of my back so that I could do it the more easily.

His hands slid down over my hips, diving into my pants and under my buttocks, and he lifted them just as effortlessly and slid my knickers down my thighs. Without being asked, I drew up first one knee, then the other; then kicked my legs free of the clinging flimsiness of the briefs I was wearing, and lay still.

He looked at me.

"What a wonder is a woman's body", he said.

"And a man's, I answered him, and slid my two hands down under his penis.

"I should not be doing this", I thought, but that was my brain speaking, and what was happening to me was something much more basic. Entirely primitive! I wanted this man. I wanted this man to have sex with me. I lusted for his body. He was no longer a pallid prisoner that had been locked up for almost half of my lifetime. He was crackling with sexual electricity. I had saved him twice. From the waters, and from the cold of death. And he had come to life again. And I wanted him. My body ached for him. My breasts pained with the ache in me, and my insides were like the vacuum of space, with an emptiness that only he could fill. I folded him into myself.

There is a phenomenon that occurs annually in the United States, in the South West, I think. A million 'Monarch' butterflies hibernate in certain forest glades for the duration of the winter. Actually, it's more like fourteen million, or twenty four million; as if anyone could count them. It is a place I want to go to sometime, not just to photograph them, but to experience them. When they mate, it must be one of the greatest acts of copulation on the planet. But it is the thought of an event beyond that, that fascinates me. When all the grubs, the caterpillars that they produce, become chrysalises and start to metamorphose, together as it were in a single act of creation, it must be as close as one can get to a proof of the existence of God.

There on that bed, I felt as if all those chrysalises metamorphosed inside me.

Maybe this didn't happen at all. Perhaps it was only a fantasy that flashed through my brain in the 'twinkling of an eye'. One of those wishes that we daydream of, and that never become a reality. If that's so, then I have committed no sin. Father, I have nothing to confess. I had no real knowledge of what I thought I was doing. It didn't really happen. For your penance, say nothing. Oh, but I wanted it to happen. I wanted it with all my heart, and my body and my soul. Say that it did happen. Say that it was real.

The photographs were real. We sat in the afternoon at a picnic bench across the road from the One Hour Photo shop in Donegal town that Ruan recommended, sat in the cold, and viewed them. There on the edge of the harbour, just downstream from the castle that's almost totally obscured by the hotels and the bank and the shops and the cafes on that side of the 'Diamond'. And we decided among the two of us, independently of Conaghan, what pictures we should email to him. We had driven to Donegal, rather than to the city, because Ruan still hoped to get an exclusive story from Owen Friel, and Owen wanted to go to Donegal, but he left us to go to a bank, and never came back.

Then Ruan drove us to his grandmother's house and I was introduced to Mary Katherine and to his Aunt Martina, and we scanned in the photographs we intended to email, and Ruan typed up his copy and the lot was sent, and I had no way out of stopping the night.

As I climbed into the big old-fashioned comfortable bed in Mary Katherine's guestroom long after midnight, I heard again, in a flashback, the rustle of the sheets as I climbed out of bed in the room in the Lakeside Hotel, and suddenly it dawned on me. The sheets were silk. We had been given the Bridal Suite. No wonder he spun the two of us so easily. And the charge between us? Was it all just static electricity? Were we just glass rods to be stroked with a silken cloth? Surely the chemistry was of a different Quantum State altogether! Sub-molecular? Maybe not. Maybe he was just a man.

CHAPTER FIVE

CONTRITION

Diary entry: April 2nd, 2001. Morning.
Jenny Stronnach's journal.

We didn't get away today, either. I don't know what Conaghan will say. Well, that's not true. It's just that I don't want to think of what he will say. Lucky we're staying with Mary Katherine. We've no expenses, therefore, for him to disapprove of.

Mary Katherine, and Ruan, were already up when I awoke this morning, about nine o'clock. The big old-fashioned bed was comfortable, but it was yesterday's happenings that had me sleep so heavily. I wondered at Ruan not also sleeping as heavily, but then realised this was his home. It wasn't just his grandmother's house; it was his. At least, it had been for the last fourteen or fifteen years. This was a house besieged by tragedy, as indeed Ruan himself was, and yet I had never known it. I suppose I had some excuse, I've worked with him – well, on the same paper as him – for only two or two and a half years now. And he is a bit younger than I. Is that why he seemed so shy, I wonder? Not wanting anyone to know his background. I looked at Mary Katherine, seeking answers. She acknowledged my look. I'm certain of that. Yet, the look she gave in return held no offer of information. Not then! Not yet, maybe.

She was a handsome woman. How old was she, I wondered? Seventy or thereabouts if Owen Friel's tape was to be believed. About right, I thought, but she could pass for ten years younger. She was that fresh. Professionally made up, she might even lose another five years, notwithstanding the strong dark hair that had long since shaded to grey. High cheekbones: That give-away of her western island ancestry. Not over tall, but carried her-self more erect than many a sixty-year old. Bold blue eyes; still undimmed. She greeted me in her native Gaelic.

"Mora dhuit, a thaisce. Tá súil agam gur chodail tu go maith. Bhfuil ocras ort? Tá braon té sa phota. Beidh sé fós te."

Ruan started to translate for me, but he didn't need to, and she shushed him.

"The girl knows fine well what I said to her, "Don't you?" she asked, and went on to say that maybe the tea was already brewing too long.

"Why don't you have a bit of a shower, and dress, while I make a fresh bit of breakfast?" and she brooked no refusal.

"Then you can accompany me down to Mass," she said, "it's at ten o'clock", and I knew there was no refusing that either.

The one task left little enough time for the other, yet we still managed to make it out the door by about ten minutes to ten, leaving the breakfast things still on the table. I paused, just before we reached the 'Espace', which was parked at the side of the house, thinking to ask if she would like me to drive. But I was swept on by the pace of her, and she sat up into the drivers seat like a teenager with a mini.

"Ruan will do the dishes" she said, "he's not coming with us. He likes to go in his own time." And she drove off down the hill.

I wanted to look at her, in daylight as it were, but you know the way it is when you are being driven along narrow country lanes, especially when they are edged with high banks and hedges; your eyes are drawn constantly to the next bend in the road. It always seems as if whoever is driving is going too fast, but there was a sureness in Mary Katherine's driving that relieved my uneasiness.

"Men," she commented, "tell you things in their own time. Women, too, sometimes."

She looked at me, taking her eyes briefly off the road. I merely looked back at her, our eyes meeting only for the instant, and said nothing.

"Yes," she said, "women, too." Then we were there.

After Mass, she delayed a while, praying some private prayers, as I made my outside into the churchyard. People were leaving, some singly, some by twos. Some stepped into cars, others walked. One couple stopped to talk to a single man, and stood on the step just outside the porch. Two, I think, went around the side of the church to where I had seen gravestones when we first drove in. After a while, they re-appeared, and walked off down the road. A little while later Mary Katherine emerged, and taking my arm, walked me around the side of the Church. She started to say something.

"You won't mind joining me…" then broke it off, and stopped in mid-step.

A figure, a man with his back to us, was standing at one of the graves. His head was bowed, and more than ordinarily there was a feeling that it was a private moment. We stood, as I thought it, respecting that moment. Then I thought to look at Mary Katherine. The assuredness I had seen in her, ever since we arrived the previous evening, was gone. Suddenly, there was a vulnerability about her; something more, even.
For a moment, I thought I recognised the figure. Thought there was something familiar about him. But I dismissed the thought. "How could there be? I was never here before." Then it struck me. The clothes were newly familiar. Newly bought, too. I hadn't looked at them too closely the previous day when Ruan returned from his shopping expedition. I was too full of confusion from what had happened to me. No, that's not right. From what I had done myself, and of my own free will. And from the maelstrom of emotions I had loosed within myself.

"Owen Friel, God save us. Have mercy on us all. God forgive you! Is it you that's standing at my daughter's grave? My daughter that's not there! My daughter that's lying where no Christian man knows. Whoever knows is no Christian. If he were, a Christian, I mean, wouldn't he tell me?"

It was Mary Katherine who had spoken. She had beaten me to his name. And it was indeed Owen Friel. I saw that when he turned around. Saw the hurt in him. Saw the tears that welled in his eyes and the glistening wet traces, like snail tracks, down his cheeks.

I moved away. This was a private moment, like no other I had ever experienced, and I had no right even to be there. But life allows us no say in such moments, and although I moved away, what was said between them followed after me, carried on the stillness of the mid-morning air. An Act of Contrition: A declaration of sorrow for all that she had suffered. Full of self-blame, of self-explanation also. Not of culpability. He said that it was not he who murdered her daughter, but another whom he came eventually to know, and that he named only as the 'Voice'. But it was not he that pulled the trigger, Patrick Friel maintained, but another still, whose face he had seen. But the first, the first man he insisted, it was he who shouted to "Shoot her." And he was powerless to stop them, even though he tried. Just as he was powerless to move fast enough on the deck of the 'Ocean Voyager' when Francis Coll -

"Your son-in-law, Mary Katherine" he said, "who is buried in this grave, and whose gravestone it is also –

"who was cut in two, virtually in my arms, and whose blood was tracked into mine by the splintered steel…."

He faltered, his emotion choking off the words even before he could utter them.

"Death made blood-brothers of us, Mary Katherine" he said, "and the vengeance I seek is his. It is what has driven me all this time. It is both the fuel and the turbo-charger that has kept me alive for fifteen solitary years. That, and the knowledge that some day I would get out, and I would know who it was that had murdered Frances. It was for that knowledge that I let myself go to prison in the first place. That, and my own guilt in involving her." But he didn't say in what.

He eventually stopped, and he and Mary Katherine held onto each other, not in an embrace, but at a distance, as it were, facing each other, each holding the top of the other's arms. As if there was an abyss between them. Then he loosed his grip and turned away. There was still a wetness of tears on his cheeks.

Mary Katherine tried to call after him, but the words failed to come. Then stifling her own tears, she recovered that firmness of voice of hers again, and her words hung in the silent air of the graveyard.

"Find my daughter's body, Owen Friel. Bring her home. Bring me peace. I don't know what hand you had in her death, and I don't know if you owe this fairly to me. But I put this burden on you. I put this 'geis' on you, this irremovable bond – you know what I mean. Bring my Frances home to me and to her dead husband."

Then she turned and walked after me to where the 'Espace' was parked. Reaching into her handbag, she handed me the keys.

"Maybe you would drive the car home for me," she said, "if you wouldn't mind."

That's what I did.

CHAPTER SIX

CONFESSION

Diary entry: April 2nd, 2001. Afternoon and evening.
Jenny Stronnach's Journal.

There was a change in the afternoon. The continental high that had given us the hard clear frost slipped away to the south, and the fringe of an Atlantic low swirled across the bay. I had never been here before to experience such a thing, but Ruan and his grandfather, Stephen, explained it, showing it to me on a weather print-out. It seems they had installed in the house a discarded piece of equipment from the 'Ocean Voyager', which they still owned, along with certain original crewmembers, Owen Friel being one of them. It wasn't as if they managed the vessel; Mary Katherine and Stephen's other daughter, Martina, did that from an office in Killybegs. But it was still a family affair. So they told me. And while Mary Katherine cleared the lunch things, the three of us sat in a window-seat as the front closed in the bay.

"How had I not seen this man the night before?" I asked myself. Like most of our kind, I was reared with the legend of 'the woman behind the man'. When first faced with it, I had failed to see 'the man behind' this woman. Even my own photographic perception betrayed me. He was already 'out the hill' when I arose this morning, tending to sheep, ewes that were lambing, and we didn't meet until lunchtime. And it was only when he bowed his head before taking his bite, and recited a simple grace, that I saw the strength in his simplicity. I knew then that I wanted to photograph this man, Stephen Coll, and his wife, Mary Katherine, before I left again for the city. After lunch I asked them if I could.

Mary Katherine had been sitting apart from us, at the table, after she had cleared away the lunch things, and had taken out what seemed to be a photo album or a scrapbook. The day's paper, which Ruan must have slipped down to the town to get while we were at Mass, was lying, still folded, on a sideboard. There was no indication that Mary Katherine had yet looked at it, but I saw Stephen spread it when he came in from the hill, and fold it back again without comment. Now, looking at the scrapbook, or whatever, she was uncharacteristically quiet.

"You are a photographer", she said to me. "Have you a good eye? What do you think of our photos?" and she half pulled back a chair and laid a hand on the seat as an invitation. I moved across and sat beside her at the table. It was indeed an album, and she turned back the broad leaves to the first page, and slid the whole thing in front of me. It was a pictorial record, much as you would get in any house, but there was a visual simplicity in the quality of the photographs, that collectively made the whole album an artistic achievement. The snaps were all black and white to start with, taken entirely in ambient light conditions. The focus on the subject was perfect. You saw exactly what the unnamed photographer wanted you to see, even to the minor details.

There was only one photograph on the first page. A contact print, I thought, from a glass plate negative. An interior, and from the detail it showed, I supposed it to have been a time exposure. I guessed it to be a snap of the room we were sitting in, before it was altered. There was a difference about the hearth, for one. A particular feature that showed was a weapon of some kind that rested on two outcropping stone pegs, one either side of, and above the mantle. Stephen moved across from the window seat, when he saw what I was looking at, to explain it to me. It was a pike, he said, that was usually kept in a place of concealment, but that had been taken out for the purposes of the photograph. And he took me 'down into the room' and showed me where it was still hidden. Making my way back into the main room again, I looked particularly at the 'cluid', which had replaced the original hearth, and noted that the two stone pegs had clearly been preserved also when the cottage was rebuilt.

"About 1920", Stephen said as he followed after me, "that's when the photograph was taken. Not much light, then," he laughed, "more like darkness visible."

He talked later about the life his parents inhabited; he, himself also, until he was already a young man. They had penny candles when times were good, rush lights with melted mutton-fat when they were not. There were occasions when they had neither. Wartime, World War Two time, that is, was a prosperous time. There was demand for the coarse wool from their black face mountain sheep, for uniforms and greatcoats, and for the meat on the hoof. Although scarce, they had paraffin for lamps and Primus stoves. Electricity came only with the Rural Electrification scheme of the 1950's, just in time for the rebuilding of the house, after Stephen's father died. The bottled gas came next and did away with paraffin, although they still kept the old lamps, for emergencies. The piped water was laid in sometime in the sixties. Stephen himself had installed it, drawing from a spring well further up the hillside.

It was Mary Katherine who told me about the house, she had such a hand in it. The traditional Donegal cottages had typically three rooms only: One room 'up', one room 'down', and a 'kitchen', a dayroom really, in between. The couple's bed – Mary Katherine looked at me – "if they were married," was curtained off in an out-shot. This was roofed with stone slabs. As a recipe for dampness, it could hardly be bettered. The main roof of the house was a rounded thatch that was laced down with a pattern of ropes, which were fastened to a necklace of stone pegs set into the wall just below the eaves. Mary Katherine changed all that.

The house I was now sitting in was clearly far bigger. It was longer, and deeper. There were still rooms 'up' and 'down', but now there were two at either end. She had retained the 'out-shot', more for tradition' sake than for use, and had accommodated the West of Ireland 'cluid' in the fire breast wall. There were later additions. A further building was raised to the rere, and connected to the house by a conservatory. The 'outshot' had been sacrificed for access to the conservatory, which served also as a passage to a bathroom and toilet in the new block. The main house had been plumbed also. One room was converted as a kitchen, and two attic rooms under the steeply pitched thatch had been converted to en-suite accommodation, each with a tiny gable window. The funny thing was, the main house was kept resolutely traditional in having only one access door, at the rere, away from the prevailing westerly gale.

In such a setting, the only way to photograph either of them, I felt, was in black and white, using only the ambient light, and I seated each of them in turn at the window seat. I posed Mary Katherine with the photo album on her knee, opened at the first page. Stephen, I merely sat in the window seat; any additional prop would have been superfluous. I thought to take the two of them together, in colour, in the conservatory, but decided to leave it for another day. I had the feeling there would be one.

When I was finished, I moved back and sat again with Mary Katherine at the table and continued looking at the pictures in the album. Stephen and Ruan reoccupied the seat at the window. Ruan had been exceptionally quiet throughout. Mary Katherine unfolded the newspaper, and looked over her shoulder at him.

"Tell us about the story in the paper" she said. "What was it like meeting him after all this time? I knew that he was getting out, you know, and was sure that is what you needed the car for. You could have told me."

She left the rest of her chiding unspoken, and cut him off quietly when he started to answer her.

"I met him myself already, you know, after Mass, standing at your mother's grave. He said he didn't kill her. Do you believe that? I don't know. I put a 'geis' on him, to find your mother's body and take her home. I'll not release him from that." And with that she was silent.

Ruan was firm in what he said:

"It is my father's grave, Mary Katherine, and it will be my mother's. When we find her and bring her home. And we will find her. I'm sure of that. I think it will be Owen Friel who will find her, and he doesn't need your 'geis' on him to drive him. But of all people, I don't think there is anyone more alone in this universe, unless it is myself, in this determination. Determination is not even the word. Desperation is closer. And I'm trying to reach out to him, because I know that without him, I have no chance of doing it by myself. There is too much that has happened to him, and to him alone, for anyone else to know what happened. He is the key, and I'll not let go of him."

I saw his grandfather, Stephen, in him at that moment. I looked at Mary Katherine, and saw that she was crying, quietly, and I didn't know if it was because of what Ruan had just said, or for her daughter whom she had never buried, or for her son-in-law whom she had. I excused myself and made my way to my room.

I slipped off my shoes and lay back on top of the bed. The murmur of conversation below in the room still reached me in snatches.

"There is a funny thing" I thought, "They have kept the original planked doors, despite changing the windows."

The windows throughout the house were double-glazed, and although they were in what I took to be the original cottage style, the frames were clearly made of PVC. The latches on the doors were themselves a give-away. There were no handles, as we understand them. No wonder I could hear much of what was being discussed below. I started to drift into a sleep, and dreamt of being in an infernally dark place. Thunderheads hung menacingly in the sky of whatever place I was at. Rain fell but did not wet me. Flashes of lightning discharged themselves everywhere and yet I never saw a distinct flash anywhere, only the reflections. Figures of people ran hither and thither. At least they seemed at first to be people; but after a while, it seemed to me they were not people at all. They were like shadows with substance. Still, they had no substance. Dark matter, that's what they were, dark matter. I started to think that they could be photographed, in the way that the dark matter in space has been photographed, and given false colours. They could be things of beauty, I thought. And then a wind blew through this place, and there was fear in it, and the dark phantasms moaned from fear, and a terror wrapped itself around me, and I tossed and twisted ……..

"Easy now."

A hand rested lightly on my arm. Firm, but reassuring.

"Easy now." The same voice again. "Easy, Jenny. I doubt you were dreaming. A bad dream! Come down to the room and have a cup of tea. Mary Katherine will make you a cup of tea."

It was Stephen. I felt safe then. He was that kind of a man. A child could stand in a gale with him and wrap two arms about his leg and be safe. The ocean of life had hurled its greatest storm against him and still he held solid against the surge. His daughter had been murdered and her body never found. I wondered what wrath he stored up against those who killed her.

"What kind of a dream was it?" he asked me, and when I told him, he stiffened slightly and said "neither soul nor flesh."

He nodded.

"I've had similar dreams myself; after Korea. And after……"

He never finished the sentence. He didn't need to.

"What's left when both body and soul are blown away. That's what you saw."

Mary Katherine made me a cup of tea and, excusing herself, left me sitting at the table. The photo album was still open at the first page and as I sipped my tea, I idly turned the pages. It was very much the story of their marriage and the start of the history of their family. The almost mirror-image likeness between the two girls, the twins, when they were young, was uncanny. The way it always is with twins. But as they grew it was clear they developed different identities, to the point where you would doubt they were twins at all. There were pictures of Francis Coll also, "naturally", I thought, and then a surprise. Pictures of Owen Friel; often in the company of the other sister, Martina. Now that I saw it, I supposed "why not?"

Martina was expected for dinner. That's what had Mary Katherine so long in the kitchen. She was doing something extra. Martina, I was told, lived closer to Killybegs, where she had a house of her own. She managed the new vessel, still named 'Ocean Voyager', from an office on the quayside. Before that, she had skippered the vessel herself, after the disaster. She wasn't the first woman skipper in Ireland: That honour belonged to Kathleen Kelly in the south coast port of Helvick. But Martina was the first to win a Skipper's (Full) Certificate that allowed her captain any size of vessel in any part of the world. And she had done just that, in the 'Ocean Voyager. I was looking forward to meeting her again. We met the previous evening, but that day was just too full to take anything extra on board. I was to be disappointed.

Martina didn't show, merely phoned. She had to go to Castletownbere. Business: Some problem affecting the vessel, which was operating off the South West Coast.

We sat late to dinner. The table talk was subdued, polite only. It was time for me to be gone, maybe for both Ruan and I to be gone, but our departure had to wait till morning. We ate slowly. The evening darkened outside. It was maybe ten o'clock, maybe half past. Lights that had been cunningly set into little mounds of rocks in the grassy hillside in front of the house switched themselves on and illuminated the house and surrounds – one could hardly call it a garden, although that is what it was. No one was paying too much attention, because this was something that happened every evening; by it self almost; the switching controlled by the ambient light. Gradually we became aware of a figure, some man, standing in front of the house. Standing just wasn't the correct word. This man was drunk and he was like a bush blowing in the wind. That peculiar state that very drunk people get themselves into, when they appear to be staggering, but never move from the one spot. Just standing upright is a struggle.

Stephen and Ruan moved closer to the window. It was Ruan who recognised him. Maybe because he had seen him back-lit before. "It's Owen Friel", he said.

"God preserve us." This was Mary Katherine.

"He's no threat", said Ruan. "God help him, he can hardly stand."

"MARY KATHERINE! STEPHEN! STEPHEN COLL."

He staggered with the effort of shouting and did a kind of a three-step to stay standing.

"I NEVER MEANT ANY HARM TO YOU OR YOUR'S."

He paused, taking his breath, gathering his thoughts with difficulty.

"AND NOT YOU RUAN. I WOULD NEVER DO ANYTHING TO HURT YOU RUAN."

It's not really possible to capture the wildness of this apparition on paper. It would be even less so with a still camera. Maybe with a movie camera; with the right lens! There is an image from the second of the James Whale 'Frankenstein' movies that comes close. Mary Katherine moved toward the door, but Stephen was ahead of her, and we watched as he rounded the corner of the building and gathered the drunken Owen with an arm around him and took him into the house.

"Make him some coffee, woman", he said, "this man needs it", and he sat him down at the table.

It was some time before he could speak. The coffee revived him though, and he rambled on more or less coherently.
"I'm sorry. Sorry", he said, "I'm not used to strong drink. Not this long while."

I looked at him. He wasn't joking. He was wrapped in some inner secret, and wouldn't have known how to joke.

"You're not fair, Mary Katherine. I don't care what you think; it's not fair. What did you put a 'geis' on me for? That's just not fair."

He paused, thinking what next to say. Nobody answered him. I think everyone knew he was too far gone to converse in any way with him. He looked at me.

"Who are you?" he asked. "Do I know you?"

"Who is she, Stephen? Why is she here? She can't be here, Stephen. I saw her blown away, Stephen, and I couldn't stop it. Her blood spattered on me, Stephen. Honest to God, it did, Mary Katherine, and I tried to prevent it, but I wasn't able to, even though I tried, and all I could do was jump through the window and get away. But I've never got away."

He slumped across the table and rested his head on an arm for a while, then lifted himself up again.

"How many times have I come into this house, Mary Katherine, bidden or unbidden? I never had call to knock on your door. How can I come in now? What happened to me? It's not the same. It can never be the same. I go to Mass, you know, even still, looking for answers, but I don't get them. I pray that prayer before communion, you know, 'Lord I am not worthy', but it doesn't reassure me. It doesn't give me 'faoiseamh'. There's no absolution in it. It's as if I never really confessed, and God knows I have. I do it every day. But it still doesn't seem to work, and I don't want to go back, but I always do. That's the way I felt coming here. I have been able to go nowhere unbidden this past fifteen years, not even beyond the door of my cell, and now that I can, I still can't. Only with drink on me."

He was sobering now, not so much from the coffee, more from whatever spectres haunted him, and he had our attention. But nothing could have prepared me for what He said next.

"I made love to her, Mary Katherine, and I tried not to. I never wanted to; I never wanted her in that way, only as a friend and the wife of a friend. But it was a comfort thing. It was that night of the funeral."

He faltered, but nobody spoke. He went on.

"It was the funeral dinner that started it. It was too much. And when she persisted in asking me why Anthony - the 'Fly', you know - hadn't turned up, and I let slip that I had found him murdered, it was too much altogether. And she asked me to take her away out of there, out of that place; and we drove back to our house and sat at the fire drinking whiskey. And my father came from the funeral; and after he went to bed in the room below, she went to bed in the room above, in my room, and I slept where I was in the bed in the 'outshot'. But she came to me, cold with loneliness and misery, in the middle of the night and climbed in beside me for warmth. Like a child seeking comfort, but she was no child. I was naked, the way I always sleep, and she was wearing only a tee shirt of mine as a shift, and she snuggled into me the way a child might."

Stephen Coll half rose from the table, as if he was going to do something, murder perhaps, and the skin prickled on the back of my neck, but the moment passed, but not unnoticed. Owen Friel saw it for what it was, but he continued.

"I won't blame you, Stephen, if you take down the pike, or you Mary Katherine, and strike me down, but I am only telling you what I have confessed so many times. That night we were just two bewildered human beings whose lives had been shattered, and a moment that neither of us wanted, happened. And I have carried the guilt of it ever since."

I looked away towards Ruan, and saw the question framed soundlessly in the man-boy's eyes.

"What about me? Did I not need comforting on that night?

Then something extraordinary happened and I can't explain it.

Before the wild figure of Owen Friel had appeared like some apparition out of the night, Stephen had been watching some programme on television; a current affairs thing; something to do with fishing, I think. The set was one of those 'flat', wide screen affairs. Expensive! It had been set into an alcove in one of the main walls of the house, above some bookshelves and didn't really fit. It just looked awkward. But the picture was live. With the appearance of Owen Friel, Stephen Coll had merely quenched the sound. Now, what was showing was the late night news, and from the images on screen, it apparently had something to do with the 'Saville' Inquiry in Derry. One of the 'new' notables, an ex-LRA activist turned politician, was being interviewed. Suddenly everyone in the room was conscious that Owen Friel was looking at the TV, and they all turned to look at it. I looked at Owen Friel. Drunk no longer, his eyes had locked onto the screen. Black lasers: that's what they were.

"The Voice." That's all he said.

"What about......? " started Stephen, "but there's no sound."

Then he stopped, as if he understood something the rest of us did not. I looked about for Ruan. That same hurt was still in his eyes, that same question:

"What about my pain?"

Then it was gone, and it was as if it had never been there.

A strategic retreat! What was it that Mao Tse Tsung wrote in his treatise on the conduct of guerrilla warfare? 'The enemy advances, you retreat; the enemy camps, you harass.' It was time for this boy-man to come off the back pedal, but I had no idea whether he was ready or not. I retreated myself, to bed.

CHAPTER SEVEN

RESOLUTION

It was time to get real, time to take charge. All my life I had been jerked around, the whole thing just a big jerk-off. Father killed in the most horrific accident ever recorded this side of the Atlantic: Mother missing, presumed murdered, this fifteen years. And I was supposed to function 'normally'. Just like any other human being. Well, I had news for them. I was through being 'normal'. I was going to be just like the rest of them. Mean. Moody. All twisted inside. Full of revenge. Hands like talons, ready to hook into everything that was going. This was the way it was every morning. And every morning I somehow put it behind me and opened the bedroom door to another day of acceptance that this was the hand that life dealt me, and I could only play it for what it was. Not this morning, though.

It wasn't yet half past five when I shook Owen Friel awake on the settle bed under the window. That was where he had spent the night, covered only with a bit of a quilt that Mary Katherine must have thrown over him.

"It's half five," I told him, "time to make a move. You've things to do today, and you need to get your head sorted. And get cleaned up."

"Is that so?" he asked "What things?"

"Be photographed," I said, "and tell us the truth. As much as you know of it. Whether you like it or not, I'm going to write it, and Conaghan is going to print it."

That startled him, but I didn't think it was what I had said, more the name, Conaghan, that did so. I quizzed him on it.

"Did you know Conaghan?" I asked him.

"The reporter?" he asked.

"He's an editor now" I told him.

"I knew him," he said, "he taped me. Twice he taped me – "

"The bastard," I said, "I was beginning to think there was another tape."

He continued seamlessly.

…. " once, in Killybegs, after the first accident, and a second time, in Dublin, after the second."

Now it was my turn to be startled.

"You didn't know about the second accident, then. I wondered about that. Not many did. Three LRA volunteers died in that one, and it was just that, an accident, and they air-brushed it from the record. They didn't want anyone to know what was going on. But I was implicated, and it was down to me. I don't know now if I should still be afraid of them, or they of me. I am another kind of a 'Typhoid Mary'. I carry death with me."

"Tell me later," I told him. "Meet us in the bar across from the Castle. In Donegal town. They've cleaned the plaster off it, and pointed the stonework. Put in Elizabethan style windows, with stone mullions. You can't mistake it. Eleven o'clock, maybe half eleven. Wait for us. We'll be there, even if we get delayed. Don't stand me up."

Then I pushed him out the door.

"That was it," I thought, "I made the start, now to wake Jenny Stronnach."

I turned away from the door. Before I had even half a step taken, the door re-opened behind me and Owen Friel was pushed back into the room. Doing the pushing was Aunt Martina.

"Where are you off to in such a rush," she asked, of nobody in particular, "and at such an early hour?"

Owen Friel had no answer. Truth was, he wasn't given a chance to answer. I was first to get my speak in.

"Jesus," I said, "I thought you were in Castletownbere. You phoned....."

I let it hang.

"Was," she answered, " I was in Castletown. Flew down yesterday, on the afternoon flight from Carrickfin. Had a car waiting in Farranfore. I was in Castletown in three hours. From Killybegs."

She caught the 'How?' on my lips.

"I got a lift back in one of the fish lorries. I bunked down in the back of the cab for four hours, until we got to Claregalway, then I spelled the driver - Jimmy Diver, I'm sure you know him - as far as Killybegs."

She was talking on the move, almost at a run. She swung towards Owen again.

"I'm glad you're out," she said, "But you've explaining to do. And I've business with you. Call me. You know where I'm at."

She hesitated then.

"No, I don't suppose you do. Things change in fifteen years. It's different now."

"Yes," he said. "Things change in fifteen years. They are different now. I'll call you. I have business with you, plans I want to talk about, and you can help me. If you want to. But I've an appointment with this man first, and I need to get my head together."

With that, he was gone. For a moment, I thought he was going to say "this boy here", but he didn't, and I appreciated that.

"Welcome back, Aunt Martina," I said, "you're some doll." Then I went in to make her some breakfast.

While it was cooking, I roused Jenny, and just kept everything hot until all three of us could sit together and plan the day. Martina could take Jenny into Killybegs. Some deepwater whitefish boats were landing, as well as blue whiting boats and mackerel boats – I had already phoned the port – and a folio of pictures would keep Conaghan happy. Would take the edge off his bark, in any case. Later, the two of them could meet us in Donegal, and meantime, I could get the story of the second tape out of Owen. Not that I said anything about any tape to either Jenny or Aunt Martina. "Not yet" I thought.

I caught up with Owen in his house, the first time I had set foot in the house since Grandfather Stephen restored the thatch after the fire. That was almost twelve years ago. Somebody fired it after Owen Friel's father died. Within days of the funeral! My grandfather felt shamed by it, that anyone would do such a thing, in his name as it were, and Stephen had redone the thatch and had the damage to the house made good at his own expense. To my knowledge, nothing was ever said to Owen Friel, then or since, and I wasn't going to tell him now. But that was the first thing he alluded to when I knocked and pushed in the door.

"Tell Stephen I thank him. About the fire I mean. It was more than I deserved, and I owe him. One more debt on top of so many."

He was sitting at a table, the only thing in the room apart from four or five chairs and an old-fashioned dresser. He had a mug of tea in front of him and a bottle of whiskey on the table. The bottle was three quarters full with the cork half in half out of it. His hair was still wet after washing and clearly hadn't been towelled too well, if at all. He rose and fetched two tumblers from the dresser. Two old-fashioned whiskey tumblers: Plain, thick glass in them. Cheap glasses, from his father's time! He poured whiskey into both of them, more than half filling them. He pushed one over to me.

"You'll have a drink," he said, "to my parents. To my father, who died with no son to wake him: I was in jail and was freed only for the funeral. You're the first to take a glass of any kind from my hand to his memory. Drink with me."

I did so. The whiskey was mellow from being so long in the bottle. A cork in a whiskey bottle! They're all screw-capped now. It must have been sitting in a press all of twenty years. But it was still whiskey, and one glass followed another even if it was on the early side of eight in the morning. I was lucky I'd had a breakfast, it absorbed some of it. But there was nothing to absorb the story, his story, my mother's story, in quite the same way. The bed where the two of them – rutted is the word, but now, now I understood how it happened, and understood – lay just behind us in the out-shot, only partly screened off. I understood, too, the sense of guilt and shame that drove him out the mountain; and the circumstances of the chance meeting with two labouring men, building workers, that gave a lift to him when he came down off the hill, over by Crove, where those famous fiddlers live; and the way it so easily happened that he set them mad with drink. The same was happening to myself.

He talked of the hundreds that came for my father's funeral, men that he knew and men that he had heard of, from all over the country. From the continent, even. But he talked, too, of the strangers, a handful of men and one woman, that nobody knew, and whom he suspected, in the shock of Anthony Killoge's death – murder, he called it, of knowing what was on the tape that Anthony Killoge had given him. Suspected that that was why they were there. And all of that was why he set out on a mad drive to Dublin; to deliver the tape to someone he knew in the Special Branch, someone from home. And he was followed.

I re-enacted that drive later this same day for Jenny Stronnach as we drove to Dublin. We met in the bar-restaurant in Donegal Town as arranged. I don't think even Aunt Martina realised how drunk I was.

We had left nothing in the bottle, had a few more as we waited for them in the bar. The photo shoot took twenty minutes only, a few shots of him standing in front of the courthouse; some profiles and head shots, in the grounds of the Castle. The difference between our drive and his was that ours was in the broad light of day; his, fifteen years ago, was a wild, moonlight ride in the frost of an October night.

They were nearing Maguire's Bridge, he told me, when he realised that the two lights that were mesmerising him, with the steadiness of them in the rear view mirror, belonged to a single car that was holding station just behind him. Clear of the village, he accelerated for Lisnaskea. What he was driving was a Peugeot pick-up truck with half a load of builder's sand. The two builder's labourers, both as drunk as himself, were sobering fast in the cab beside him. The blindness of the narrow road favoured him. Through Lisnaskea, he held steady for Newtownbutler, and continued straight on, for Wattle Bridge and Cavan.

This was then an 'unapproved' road. Open to traffic, but not approved for travel between Northern Ireland and the 'South' – the Republic. Halfway along it's five-mile length, the road skirted a tiny lake with an even smaller wooded islet in it, making an S-bend around it. Local Loyalists had fastened a flag on a light stick to the topmost branch of the tallest tree, proclaiming their eternal defiance, their dominance, their insecurity, their fear. It was a white flag with a red cross on it and the red hand of Ulster at it's centre, the flag of the short-lived Vanguard Party. I remembered it myself.

The road at this point crosses a mudflow and the surface is prone to shear, and for this reason, the road has for years past been tarmacadamed. That night, it carried a generous skim of ice. Inexplicably, the pursuing car attempted to overtake.

"Jesus, they've guns" shouted one of the workmen, sober now.

Owen Friel hit the brakes and lost it instantly. The Peugeot truck sideswiped the overtaking car and threw it forward into a spin, the Peugeot itself following in an almost graceful pirouette behind it. One last touch of car bodies and the car tumbled across the verge to the left and hit a tree. The truck performed a bit of a wobble, straightened up and raced on into the night. Behind them, a trickle of spilt petrol ignited. A mile and a half on, at the checkpoint, a nervous squaddie with self-preservation on his mind recognised drunken men for what they were and waved them on. They didn't hesitate.

I had been explaining all this; the events as real as if I had myself been part of them, the bright midday light darkest night, illuminated only by a half moon. Towns and villages were no more than clapboard cut-outs, as false as Hollywood scenery. My voice was the only voice, an un-interruptible narration. We were approaching the place where the original checkpoint stood, on a reasonably straight stretch of bumpy road. I turned to look at Stronnach and couldn't believe how pale she looked. Her two hands were clasped one above the other on the strap of her seat belt.

"How far have we come?" she asked.

"About fifty, maybe sixty miles." I answered.

"In fifty three minutes!" she responded. "Jesus" she whispered, "how did we not kill anyone?"

Shocked, I slowed the car. "This is…" I started to say, but she got her question in ahead of me.

"What of your mother, and what of that IRA man Owen Friel seemed so focused on, last night, on the television?"

"LRA", I corrected her, "Liberation Republican Army. Same breed, by a different name."

Then I broke down. I unfastened my two hands from the steering wheel and clenched my fists. I held the wheel only with my wrists, then slowed and stopped the car, pulling it over in front of a burnt-out Orange Hall. My whole body curled up in a spasm and I remembered only keeling over across the gear shift.

It was twenty minutes before I came round, so she said. The first thing I saw was the pale face of her leaning over me as I heard, as if from a distance, the sound of someone calling my name: "Ruan. Ruan."

The answer to her double question oozed out of me.

"McMenamy. Ernan McMenamy. Feted now in Washington, and Judas-kissed in Dublin and London. One of the architects of the 'Peace Process'! Owen Friel calls him 'The Voice'. He was the one. Owen Friel says he was the one who gave the order to shoot her. After they were hijacked. That's what he said. Who am I to know? Jesus God, how am I to know?"

CHAPTER EIGHT

REVELATION

I was exhausted and slipped back into sleep again. I must have dozed the better part of an hour there in the car alongside the burnt-out Orange Hall. When I awoke, the sun had lowered considerably in the afternoon sky. My mouth tasted like shit, and I got out of the car and relieved myself against the back wheel, on the blind side. Jenny Stronnach was sitting some thirty yards away, on the parapet of the bridge. I walked over to her and leaned against the wall. Her feet dangled over the water, and it struck me that she trusted me. Another sitting vulnerably like that would have swung her legs back over the wall and slid to the ground. I felt comfortable beside her.

There was some difference between this 'Wattle Bridge' and that other one, 'Baile Atha Cliath', that by some error of history was cross-named Dublin – literally the 'Black Pool'. Here there were not more than five houses in all, two of them neatly kept farmhouses edging the road on the other side of the bridge.

"Peaceful, isn't it" I said.

"It's navigable all the way from here almost to the sea," I continued, "that's more than fifty miles away."

I waved at the river that flowed underneath, "only a tributary," I told her, "the Erne itself is a little further to the west. This is the 'Finn', I think, and it's also one end of the Ulster Canal. That's not used anymore." Then, forgetting that I had already pointed out the place where the original army checkpoint stood, I told her again, and pointed to an imaginary spot, just out of sight, around the bend.

"I used pass it often," I said, "travelling up and down to school. I was sent to boarding school, you know, and spent another couple of years at the School of Journalism, in Rathmines. That was before they built the 'fort apache' on the hill."

I got confused then, and made a poor job of explaining that it was the first checkpoint that came before the frontier style fortification on a rise of a hill about half a mile back, and before my stint at the School of Journalism. The fortification was one of twelve that were built along the land border between Northern Ireland and the Republic, or 'The State' as the Northern Ireland ones called it. The forts, which in most cases incorporated two high surveillance towers, for triangulation purposes, I was sure, and were loaded with all sort of high-tech equipment, had almost all been dismantled as part of the 'Peace Process'. Lives, too, had been dismantled.

In this county of Fermanagh, an IRA murder squad targeted and killed more than two dozen people who were in each instance the sole heir to the family land.

For more than fifteen hundred years, dominance and power were coveted and disputed at almost every generation. The broad, slow flowing tributaries, and the two great lakes of the Erne itself, formed both a passage from the sea to the hinterland and an East-West barrier of strategic importance. And if alliances were made, they lasted only until one or other of the parties reached home and started to think they hadn't got enough in the bargain. That was the darkness at the heart of this seemingly peaceful and beautiful land. Neither side gave or accepted trust. Only in the aftermath of the plantations, and after the final bloody suppression of the 'native' – Catholic – Irish in the business of 1798, was there a golden age of peace and a growth of prosperity. But it wasn't a shared prosperity, and people who never agreed with one another for more than a single generation at a time, unified in resentment of those they considered usurpers.

"What's with the history lesson," Jenny Stronnach remarked when I said as much to her, "where do you get it from, Mary Katherine?"

"Stephen", I answered, "my grandfather, Stephen. He's the history buff. Mary Katherine, too, I suppose. All you have to do is look at all the books in the house. There are shelves of them in every room."

Not far from where we were standing, an old apple orchard had been cleared, the trunks cut down, and the branches trimmed and gathered into piles for burning. It was symptomatic of the new regime in this year of two thousand and one: Every reminder of what was there before was to be gathered into bundles to burn. And yet, this individual thing was no more than the clearance of an orchard of old trees long past their best.

On one of our journeys to Dublin, Mary Katherine had stopped to enquire if she could buy some of the cooking apples, and also to ask what variety were the all-over scarlet apples that grew on one particular tree adjacent to the road.

"Bloody Butchers". That's what the woman called them. An old variety planted by her father, she said.

What an extraordinary name, I thought then.

"Bloody butchers." That's what I told Jenny Stronnach as we stood there at Wattle Bridge. "Two bloody butchers. One of them shouted *'Shoot her. Shoot the bitch.'* And the other pulled the trigger."

That's what Owen Friel told me, earlier this very morning. That's why I was so mad with drink. I drank to get drunk, to wipe out the pain, to obliterate whatever he said. And he drank to deafen himself to the words that he spoke. But the whiskey worked for neither of us. Certainly it made us drunk, but it cleared the receptors in our brains of any other thoughts. No other image, except the images his memory poured out for me, was retained. It was, again, as if I had been there myself.

The two builder's labourers that he had virtually hijacked, crept out of the hotel in the early hours of the morning – Owen Friel had booked all of them into 'The Fitzwilliam', one of the city's classiest hotels;

seemingly headed for home, and were never seen again. Not a trace of them, or of the Peugeot pick-up truck, was ever found. It was as if they had never existed.

Owen Friel delivered the video recording to his contact, a Special Branch detective named Martin Brennan, but when the strangers that had appeared at the funeral, including the woman, turned up in the hotel also as guests, he phoned my mother to take his car and come and collect him.

"What was on the video tape," I asked him, "that made it so special?"

"Darkness visible" he answered me. *"At just one spot in the recording, something extraordinary happened. The murkiness of the underwater images became illuminated in a manner that I never saw in my life before. Everything was still dark, just as you might expect at the depth we were fishing and filming."*

The phrase 'darkness visible' bugged me. I couldn't think where I had heard it before. Then it came to me: Stephen had used it to describe the light back in the nineteen twenties, when the old house was photographed inside. I let the thought go and explained what Owen Friel was talking about for Jenny Stronnach:

You lose the light at six hundred feet. That's a hundred fathoms down. They were fishing on the deep edge, maybe a hundred and fifty fathoms deep. The blackness should have been absolute. But it wasn't. The actual words Owen Friel used were:

"It was like looking through the eyes of God!"

Then he continued:

"Suddenly, we could see everything that was down there; bridles, meshes, frame ropes; as if we were looking at them in broad daylight, and yet it was still dark, black even. And there was something else: The hull of an enormous submarine. That was all. I guess that's when it happened. That's when your father died."

"Yes," said Jenny Stronnach, picking me up on my narrative, "your father! Tell me about your father."

I looked at her, a long, staring look, but said nothing; not in words, at any rate. This was not about my father. He was a fisherman. Death is the price fishermen pay for the beauty and the wonder and the mystery of being at sea – and for the wealth. Usually it is a crewman who pays. On this one searing occasion it was the skipper. It just happened he was my father. If Jenny Stronnach could not pick up on that, I couldn't help her.

"This is about my mother," I told her. "She was murdered to her face."

That was the story I wanted from Owen Friel. That was why I quizzed him.

"But, my mother. What about my mother?" I asked him.

"We were hijacked. We had cleared the army checkpoint at Wattle Bridge,"

– where we are now standing, I said to Jenny Stronnach –

"and although we were nervous, we thought nothing of it, further along the road, when we were flashed down again by what we thought were soldiers on patrol. That was common at the time. But they weren't soldiers. Not the Queen' soldiers, at any rate. The Queen's soldiers didn't wear balaclavas and carry Kalashnikovs."

I stumbled in the re-telling then, just as Owen Friel himself had stumbled in the telling, in his house, earlier this same morning. The words were just too hard to get out. I waved a hand away towards the Northwest.

"Away over there, forty miles from here, somewhere in that triangle between the Lower Lake and the Ballinahown road that we drove out along earlier, that's where they took them,"

… "that's what," I said to Jenny Stronnach, there on the bridge,

… "he thinks."

"He thinks!" she echoed.

"He thinks. He doesn't know, for sure."

"He thinks", I said yet again. "I mean, how could he know? They were blindfolded; their eyes were taped over; and their hands were taped together behind their backs. That's what he told me."

"He knows what happened afterwards, doesn't he?" she asked. "He escaped, didn't he?"

Three whole days they kept them. They were questioned and roughed up, daily and nightly, although, as they were kept separately in completely darkened rooms, they had no way of judging the passage of time and no chance of connecting with reality; even with each other. Each could hear when the other was being abused, though, but that only served to make it worse. What their captors were after, seemingly, was the videotape that Owen Friel had already handed on to Martin Brennan. How they knew of it was never explained, and, Owen conjectured, could only link back to whatever inadvertent disclosure led to Anthony Killogue's death. This, he said, he figured out at the time, and felt that as long as he disclosed nothing, they had some hope of living at least one more day.

Inevitably, though, the strain told on their inquisitors also. One of them, a young woman, allowed herself to be distracted when the sounds of Frances – my mother – being abused, and of her defiance, became too harrowing, and Owen Friel was able to slip his legs back over the binding on his wrists. Then, when a voice – 'The Voice', he called it – shouted out "Shoot the bitch. Fucking shoot her!" he hurled himself at his captor, his warder, and slammed both her and himself through the adjoining door.

An old door, he said, it carried away before them, crashing off the hinges. He had a glimpse, only, of a stocky, red-haired man holding a handgun, and was aware of him shooting. Shooting in his direction. Then he felt the impact, once, twice, a third time, of bullets hitting the woman, and he threw her forward at the gunman. The man with the gun continued to fire, and he realised that the bullets, now, were impacting a different target, another woman, Frances, to his left. Turning to look, he saw a final bullet hit the middle of her face, and knew that the spatters of blood, flesh and bone that landed on him were the last he would ever know of Frances Coll, and with one final effort hurled himself at the blacked out window. The obscured frame and glass splintered away before him, and he landed on a rusty, corrugated tin roof that yielded under him and broke his fall. Tumbling off it, he fell heavily to the ground, and, desperately regaining his feet, raced off into the darkness.

I looked down at the surface of the river flowing anonymously beneath us, looking for a blackness, an amnesia, into which to fall, but the surface reflected only the blue and white of an afternoon sky. I lifted my hands and extended them at arms length over the water, pointing, the way a child might, with both arms together, towards that other anonymous spot, forty or forty five or whatever miles away, to where all this happened. And it was no consolation that I knew that somewhere, 'over there', my mother died. Brutally done to death. No consolation whatsoever. I cried.

Eventually, I let Jenny Stronnach lead me back to the car, and we resumed our journey to Dublin.

CHAPTER NINE

THE THIRD DAY; MAGIC NUMBERS

Jenny Stronnach's Journal.

Three day's ago, I scarcely knew these people existed. Now I'm both a co-conspirator and a passenger on the roller coaster of their lives. They can't get off. I'm very afraid I can't get off, either. The question is; do I want to get off? It's as if I had discovered a century-old cache of photographic plates, one of those fortuitous finds one occasionally reads about, portraying a time and a place that no longer exists. Only these events that I have been made privy to, happened only sixteen years ago. One might almost say 'now'. And the place is 'here'. Wherever it's at, it's here. And I've become part of it. Jesus!

Three days! Three days are not enough. How can I make sense of it in only three days? A cache of old plates would take weeks of study to take everything out of them, might take years, even. They would have to be put into context, to be researched. Places would need to be rediscovered, faces and people identified, experts on the period consulted. That's it. It would need an expert. The right kind of expert. An academic, intellectual kind of an expert. A crossword-puzzle kind of an expert. One who could find alternative meanings in the clues and be skilled at picking the right answer. But I'm not a crossword puzzle solver. I'm a photographer. I take pictures. That's what I do, I take pictures. I freeze time. I encapsulate the moment in a microns thin film of colour, or of black and white, making it instantly an aide-memoire of the past. A dried leaf by which to remember the tree. Not even as substantial as an insect preserved in amber.

I can capture character, though, and emotion. The face is not masque enough to hide the thoughts all the time. The vizard slips, and the image of the soul reveals itself in those off-guard moments, and my eyes click on them. That's my talent, my stock in trade. I capture it on camera, maybe only once in a hundred shots, but I get it. Sometimes I'm better, though; I get one in five, or one in three, all printable. And

I get them in a run. It's like hitting a magic number. Every third one is good, or every fifth or seventh.

It becomes a self-fulfilling axiom. It's a funny thing though, the numbers seem always to be prime numbers; three; seven; eleven; thirteen. Or multiples of them. Maybe I'm just downright superstitious. If so, I'm not on my own. Others were there before me. Jonah was three days in the belly of the whale. That's appropriate, if that taped interview of Conaghan's tells it true. Nuclear submarines, Christ! Christ himself was three days in the tomb; well at least he rose again on the third day. I feel a bit like that myself, as if I'm just rising out of the tomb. I'm drained. But my pictures were good. About one in three, I reckon. There it is, that magical three again.

Three had to be the first magic number. One, on it's own, was just the individual self. What could one do? Nothing, except masturbate, like the Pharoahs! Isn't that what those 'dirty pictures' on the walls of their temples show? Two? Two is just two ones together. Three is the magic that was produced by two selves when a child appeared, born out of a night of pain, and that needed explanation. So, three became the first 'magic' number. It's as simple as that, I reckon. The mathematics came later, and the myths of creation. The Torah and the Bible record that it took God three days to pronounce that the seas be parted; and dry land and all the self-seeding fruits of the earth be made. That's not quite how it tells it, but it amounts to the same, and the whole job, including man in his image, "male and female", was completed in six days – the first multiple of three. And then God created the second magical number. He took a day off, and, adding it to the six, created seven.

But three is my favourite magic number. It's the one that works best for me, and that's where the problem lies. There are two many threes and multiples of three in this present business: Owen and Stephen and Ruan, Mary Katherine and Martina and myself! That's the thing. I'm in there. Am I in a triangle also, between Ruan and Owen? I think Ruan fancies me, but is it just the age he's at, where all women exist to be made love to, and where having a woman is still a mystery to him. And Owen that ravished me, and that I said 'Yes, Yes, Yes' in the depth of my soul to, and that since has scarcely recognised me. And then there are the dead, Francis and Frances, and Anthony Killoge, yet another three; and the IRA or LRA or whatever, how many of them were killed? How many more must die?

That's the terrible certainty. Others will die. I don't know who they will be, yet. Those Owen Friel calls 'The Face' and 'The Voice', and anyone else that gets in the way of his mission of revenge. Is that all that drives him, I wonder? Is there a real person inside that ball of anger he inhabits? Is it a ball of anger? Or is it one of hurt? The glistening streaks on his cheeks in the graveyard were real, but so was the despair when Mary Katherine put the 'geis' on him. It's as if he thought it was an impossible thing. She is something else, and Stephen is. When he put his hand on my arm as we sat in the window seat, he explaining the weather chart to me, I could feel the strength in him, that 'inner person', even in something so mundane as an explanation of 'occluded fronts'.

But the pattern of threes still bothers me. Who else is going to die besides the 'Face' and the 'Voice'? Was there another involved in Frances' murder, someone even Owen doesn't know about? I feel it. And what of the police: Did some of them 'fit' Owen up? And what of Conaghan, what's his game: Just an editor? What if the CIA were in on all of this, or the Russians? Now, there's a thought. I'm too tired right now, though. I'm going to sleep. Tomorrow is another day. Let it bring it's own package.

CHAPTER TEN

WHERE NOW?

For a while, everything became almost normal. In the run-up to Easter, the Irish teachers' unions prepared for their annual conferences. The most powerful of them was locked in a confrontation with Government, and seemed determined to tear down the existing structures in an argument about pay and recognition. An internal power struggle was talked about privately, but few seemed willing to go 'on the record' for publication. Enough, one would think, to keep any ordinary journalist busy. But that was overlaid with the havoc that a Foot and Mouth epidemic, and the mishandling of control measures was having in Britain. Several outbreaks of the disease in Northern Ireland and a single outbreak in the Republic highlighted the extent of animal smuggling from the UK mainland, via the North, and between the two Irish States, in what was clearly a major VAT scam. The most disturbing aspect, though, was the ambience of paramilitary involvement. There were 'no go' areas, even for the essentially nationalist Northern Ireland Minister of Agriculture.

All this was happening against a much broader sweep of events. In England, the 'New Labour' government of Tony Blair was pitching for re-election. In it's first term in office it had established a devolved Parliament for Scotland and an Assembly for Wales, and, with the personal involvement of a Democrat President of the United States, had arm-twisted a reluctant accommodation between the warring factions within Northern Ireland. The succession of Irish Prime Ministers in the South were happy to jump aboard, sensing a 'final solution' to the 'Irish Question', each determined that the glory be theirs. They had grown practised in their arrogance. The Irish economy was so successful that the Irish Finance Minister felt he could lecture Europe on economics, forgetting that Europe had only a while past splurged eight billion in subsidies on Ireland. Ireland had even been elected onto the Security Council of the United Nations, a triumph for both the country, and the Ambassador to the UN, Richard

Ryan, who achieved it. But, in an unprecedented move, the national Irish television service, RTE, broadcast a programme, drawing on Government documents only just released under the 'thirty year' rule, dealing with the events of 'The Arms Trial', a scandal from 1970. As I said, everything became almost normal.

Conaghan was in his element.

Then, the Chinese Peoples Republic succeeded in downing an American spy plane, which had to land on Chinese territory. The new President of the United States was a Republican. The Cold War came to life again. I knew now what it was that started all this, why it was that my father died. 'Normal' things didn't count anymore.

It almost seemed as if Conaghan was avoiding me. Ten minutes only, he gave us, Stronnach and I, before asking if I would excuse them, there was something he wanted to talk to Jenny about. I slammed the door behind me. I was both mad, and jealous.

Easter was never a good time for me. Where others took hope from the mystery of the risen Christ, or, if they were agnostic, pleasure in the rebirth of nature, I found it no different from any other time; I had to claw my way into life every morning. Nobody's life had been fucked up like mine; my childhood ended when I was seven. Ever since, I was an adult in an adult's world. I had to be. For seven years I had someone to hate - Owen Friel - then, when I figured out that there was more to the events of that year of '85, I went to visit him, in prison. Mary Katherine never knew about it, but Stephen did, almost as soon as it happened.

I mitched from boarding school, and hitchhiked to Portlaoise. Someone at the Prison took pity on me and let me in. Maybe they took pity on Owen Friel also; he had only three visitors after his father died, my Grandfather Stephen, Mary Katherine and, unbeknownst to all of us, Aunt Martina. Stephen had visited him to set him straight on the attempted burning of his father's house, and to apologise for it seemingly being done in his, i.e. Stephen's name. Mary Katherine, never one to give up on any pupil of hers, took with her application papers for 'The Open University' when she visited him. That was after the Open University extended it's operations to the Republic, and she set the challenge for him by saying that she didn't care if he tried it or not, he could rot in hell for all she cared. But she could not hide the tears, and they were not all for Frances. I'm certain Stephen had a hand in it also. But my visit was my own business.

"You owe it to me" I said to him. "You are my Godfather. You owe me the truth. I can't go on, hating someone blindly, it's burning me up. I must be clear. Either you did it, in which case I will surely kill you, or you didn't. In that case, I will kill whoever did. You tell me."

And when he couldn't tell me that he had killed her, I knew that he had not. It was as simple as that. I needed no court of law, no flawed statement, no evidence of any secret agenda, to convince me. I knew. And now, nine years on from that single meeting in a visitor's room in Portlaoise Prison, I knew who had killed my mother, both who killed her, and who gave the order to shoot. And it mattered nothing to me that both men were now Ministers in Her Majesty's Assembly in Northern Ireland, as far as I was concerned, both were 'Dead Men Walking'.

The cross was no lighter, though. You would imagine that knowing, finally, who it was that had killed my mother, might have eased the burden, might have lightened the load. You would have imagined wrongly. Life still felt as if my hands were both shackled to a great beam, laid like a yoke across my shoulders, and my mission in life was to search out a tree or a shaft with great iron brackets into which the beam could be set. A modern day Christ! I envied Christ. He had the promise of resurrection, someone was even found to help him. I had no one. And I hungered for someone; someone to talk to, to get involved with, to generate friendship with, to have an affair with, someone like Jenny Stronnach. It wasn't only that I lost my childhood. Because I became so instantly an adult, I had no adolescence either. I wasn't practised in the easy phrases of flirtation, and had no easy confidence or ability with young women. I think that's why I was jealous of Conaghan. He was like the Centurion in the Bible story, "and I say to a man, 'do this', and he doth it."

Conaghan said to Jenny Stronnach, "Go to Galway." and she went. I exploded in the corridor the same day: "It's not fucking fair." Conaghan heard me, and I got sent north again, to County Louth, to report on the Foot and Mouth outbreak. I was dismissed. As I was leaving, though, he called after me:

"You might take a run across the Border, into the North, to County Armagh, while you're at it."

I was turning away when he mentioned a date and a place and a time slot, and, for a second, thought I had misheard. In such a place it was the locals who had the franchise on asking questions, and most strangers came away with the distinct impression that they preferred not to have to exercise their franchise at all. But there was something in the way he had said it that made me take heed of it. And, on the day, and at approximately the right time, I slowed at a cross roads on an unfamiliar country lane, and was lucky not to be cut out of it by a military style convoy of vehicles, that sped, left to right, across my path.

"Jesus!" I said.

"Jesus!" I said a second time, when I realised just who it was I had seen in the back of the second car. It was a convoy. Not military, Ministerial! The man sitting in the back of the second car was the man that Owen Friel claimed killed my Mother.

"Jesus!" I said, a third time. "How the fuck did Conaghan know? What's his part in all this?" Then I gunned the car, and spun the wheel, and gave chase. But my chase didn't last long, only as far as the next crossroads. Two cars, with darkened glass in all windows except the windscreens, pulled across the road in front of me and stopped.

"Jesus!" I said, a fourth time, as I braked frantically. "The fucking IRA."

But if it was the man, it was not the IRA, it was the LRA.

"Same fucking difference", I parroted.

That's not what I said when I wound down the window, though. The two heavies that, by now, were standing either side of where I had stopped, looked as if they could easily lift the car bodily from the road, and turn it around if they so wished. I behaved as if I would never put them to so much trouble. I feigned innocence.

"Wasn't that just…..?"

I deliberately left the sentence unfinished.

"Yes. Well, maybe not. You might have been mistaken." One of them answered.

"Yes, I'm sure you were mistaken." This was the second one. "It's a poor road to be in a hurry on, in any case."

"You could have an accident. You could get hurt." This was the first one again.

I marvelled that either of them could speak, but didn't say as much. I was being nasty, the way most people can be, for internal consumption. A mechanism for excusing our own cowardice. I allowed myself to be guided back along the road I had just driven down at such a lick, and promised myself "next time!"

"Where now?" I thought, and mentally turned for Killybegs. "It's time to check in with Aunt Martina, and with Owen Friel. There's more, yet, that they haven't told me." But I thought better of it. I needed first, to check what more Conaghan could tell me, and I needed an ally to tackle Conaghan. There was only one in the world I felt was a potential ally to me at this time, and she was in Galway. So, for more than the one reason, I headed first for Cavan, and stopping there only long enough to text message her mobile that I would meet her for dinner at eight in the Great Southern, journeyed on to destiny, and a date with Jenny Stronnach.

CHAPTER ELEVEN

OTHER ROADS, DIFFERENT ENCOUNTERS

It was a poor road from Cavan to Longford, one I had never driven on before, and I found myself trying to sing, to relieve the tedium of the journey. I wasn't really a Trad and Ballad man; I spent too many years in boarding school away from Donegal to be infected with that. And I wasn't really a U2 fan either, they were before my time, and in any case, they were all about saving the world, and I only wanted to save myself. But for all of that, the verse that kept repeating itself over and over again in my mind, went:

"I've been waiting… such a long time…..", a Eurovision ballad.

I grew annoyed with myself, and hurled the car along the road, totally heedless of any traffic that might be coming. Granard, Longford, then across the Shannon at Lanesborough, on and on I sped, skirting Roscommon town centre, then turned for Ballygar and Moylough. The final run took me onto the Tuam road, through that strangely named Irish-speaking enclave, Claregalway, then on into the city, Galway, already brightening itself for the evening.

I was early, and being lucky enough to get a handy parking place, just sat waiting in the bar, not knowing if she would show. I nursed a brandy and a coffee. The dregs of the coffee were cold and I was debating with myself whether I should order another, when a frizzy, ginger-blonde head of hair was poked through the doorway, and those greeny-grey hazel eyes scanned the room. They brightened in a brief smile of recognition, then darkened somewhat, and the brow over them crinkled in a frown.

"She's wondering what the hell I'm doing here" I thought, and rose to meet her. I took her arm.

"Let's get out of here," I said, "there are other restaurants in Barna or Spiddal. They're smaller, more intimate."

"Jesus!" she said, and she looked around. "I've only just got here. Is some one after you? The CIA or the IRA? What's the panic? I've only just got here. And intimate, is it? Do you know what comes first? 'Hello!' comes first. Hello Jenny, nice to see you comes first."

I got a word in edgeways. "Hello!" I said. "Hello Jenny!" I said. "Nice to see you!" I said. "I'm really pleased you could make it." I said. "Thanks" I said. "Now let's cut the crap," I said, "there's a really nice restaurant out in Spiddal, and we'd need to be moving if we want to get a table."

She laughed at that, and we left. On the way to Spiddal in the car, I filled her in on the extraordinary co-incidence of my meeting that particular cavalcade of cars on a back road in County Armagh, when what had me there in the first place was a cryptic direction from Conaghan.

"What the fuck is his part in all of this?" I asked her, and apologised for the bad language. I was always clean spoken, but the events of the past couple of weeks had pushed me over an edge, and I knew it. More than the gates of a prison opened on that morning of April the first. That was another thing that Conaghan was au fait with, beforehand. He seemed almost a Biblical prophet, always there with advance information; isn't that what prophecy is? But what the fuck was his part in all of this?

I had no answer, no more had I any idea what Andrew Brodie, the man that Owen Friel said shot my mother, was doing in an obscure corner of County Armagh. He was an enigma in his own right. Born with an ambiguous name, one that sounded more Scottish, and therefore, by implication, Unionist, than might normally be encountered in the Nationalist community, he succeeded in maintaining a relative obscurity for almost twenty years of the 'Troubles'. Then it increasingly became clear just how critically he was involved, and how powerful. He put his head above the parapet and played a major role in all the political negotiations since, seemingly as second in command, although I had my personal doubts about that.

In the College of Journalism, I had taken Northern Ireland Studies as my major subject in my final year, and had postulated in my thesis that he was the real power behind the titular head, Ernan McMenamy. His present position married the Ministry of Reform and National Reconstruction to his Party post of deputy leader.

I spoke nothing of this to Jenny Stronnach. I wanted her as an ally to challenge Conaghan, and needed her backup to persuade him to run a major series on Owen Friel's guilt or innocence. But I also needed to separate my feelings for her from my quite deliberate determination to use anybody and anything, to get to the man who had murdered my mother, whoever he might be. But the intensity of that dark passion burned me up, and on this evening I tried to close it down.

Inside in the restaurant, we sat at a table for two, set against a darkly painted wall and our knees meshed intimately under the table. The tingle of pleasure that this afforded lightened my spirits, and I talked of my hunger to be 'ordinary', to be able to sit in restaurant such as this, with a companion such as her, and carry no more burden than swallows in the summer air. And for a short space of time, I didn't. She wondered at my familiarity with Galway and Spiddal and was curious as to how I acquired it.

"But I've been coming here since I was a child," I answered, "well, passing through in any case."

I told her then of being brought as a child to visit 'Aunts'- really aunts of my mother, sisters of Mary Katherine, and 'Uncles', back west in the islands, and how, in all the years at college, I came on summer holidays just to be anonymous. She didn't grasp what I meant, not at first, and I had to explain that it was only in the Islands that I could feel I was just another person. I wasn't Ruan Coll, whose 'Father was killed', and whose 'Mother was murdered'. I was just 'Ruan'. At home, I couldn't get away from it; everyone from Killybegs to Malin

Head knew. And at school, the other boarders picked up on it, the way boys do, and sensing about me the aura of an avenging angel, kept a distance from me. Only in the Islands, for a single month every year, was I free.

It's marvellous what freedom means for a boy. To go along with older fellows and with men, carrying a canvas currach down to the shore, three backs hunched underneath it, like a beetle, then twirl it in midair so it wouldn't get damaged against the stones – 'duirlins' – of the beach, and lower it into the water. No scarab of ancient Egypt ever metamorphosed like that. Then the launching, and me, as a boy being hooshed aboard first, and given the middle oars to row, as a challenge.

Rowing any currach, even as part of a team, is a challenge at anytime, because they are contrary craft. They have no keel and seek to crab away sideways either to port or starboard. But in mastering the technique necessary to control our passage, I learned also to master myself. It became for me, something elemental.

There is no feeling more elemental than hauling a lobster pot in the dusk, or in the early morning, the coarse black or orange netting slippery with a festoon of weed, and glimpsing through the crystal clear water the dark back and lighter, mottled sides of the 'blue' lobster. 'Lospers', the Aran men call them.

Our men, although they were from the Islands, were Connemara men and fished in the Sound, not like the Aran men who fished along the blue-black cliffs at the back of the big island. Sometimes, when our pots were shot 'too wide', out on the sand, or too close, and in on the weedy stones, we got nothing but crabs; hen crabs off on the sand, and predominantly cock crabs on the stones. They were called 'red' crabs, but they were more often a deep purple than the browny-red they turned when cooked.

Occasionally we hauled great red crawfish, but they were scarce, and we usually went offshore to where the banks of 'soft' kelp – oar-weed – grew, to get them. But it wasn't what we got that was material to me, it was the sense of a blameless self that I took back with me, and an acceptance of self by others whom I respected that transferred year by year to me. It was like growing up in instalments.

"What a beautiful way to grow up!"

That's what Jenny Stronnach said when I had finished my attempts to explain what this place meant to me, and I shrivelled when I heard it, thinking she was, perhaps, mocking me. But when I realised she was genuine, I suggested we could drive back west, - "It would only take about thirty five minutes." I said, - and I could take her out in the morning. One of the grandaunts could put us up, I suggested.

She thought on it for a moment, then answered; "I have a better suggestion."

Her suggestion was that I should drive her back to where she was stopping, in one of the hotels in Salthill – that's just on the edge of the city, along the coast road. She knew, or guessed that I had not booked in anywhere, and said that I didn't need to, she had a perfectly good bed. So she had, and that night I was tutored in the final instalment of a man's growing up – I was given no choice in the matter - and before morning had revised the lesson three times.

CHAPTER TWELVE

CLOSE YOUR EYES!

Diary: Fourth Ruan Coll entry.
Jenny Stronnach's journal.

I never knew any man to lose his inhibitions so quickly. Definitely a virgin! He had to be. I saw that the way he turned his back to me when he pulled his trousers on in the hotel down by the lake on the Shannon. He was embarrassed that I saw him, then. He was embarrassed in the hotel room in Salthill, also. He was shy. Shy but willing, like a bride in bed: that's what old Bessie used to say. Bessie that used help Mother about the house. But he has a gorgeous body. And when he turned; those buns!! I feel my hands on them, yet.

He was eager, though. We were only through the door when he wanted to kiss me. I let him. I did more than that. Aided and abetted, your Honour. Yes, your Honour. I stuck my tongue down his throat, your Honour. I freely admit it, your Honour. I sucked his face off, your Honour. Am I guilty, your Honour? I enjoyed it, your Honour. I took pleasure in it. Say I took pleasure in it: I took pleasure in it, your Honour. And when we had pleasured ourselves so much, we stopped; well not so much stopped as paused. And do you know what he said to me, then?

"Close your eyes!"

That's what he said to me.

"Close your eyes!"

And because I was a good girl, because I wanted to, no matter what, I closed my eyes, and waited.

I waited. Eyes closed, I waited. Didn't know what he was going to do. Didn't know why my eyes had to be closed. Then his hands loosened my coat and slid the two sleeves down my arms and I felt a gentle tug at the back, and it slipped clear of me. It didn't fall on the floor. He must have caught it and thrown it. I heard the so, so soft whoosh as it fell on a bed. Then his fingers were opening the buttons on my blouse, all the way down. It's funny, that. He started at the top, and went all the way down. I normally start at the bottom. When all the buttons had been unfastened, he opened my blouse. He paused then. I guess he was looking at me. I started to say something, but he put his finger across my lips. "Shsss," he said, and kissed me, gently, as he took his finger from my lips. Then, he appeared to walk away.

I almost opened my eyes. I wanted to. He must have sensed the urge in me.

"Keep your eyes closed, still," he said, "I'll tell you when to open them."

His voice gave him away. He had moved around behind me. I marvelled that he could move so quietly. I didn't even feel him move. I felt his hands on the back of my bra, though; investigating; feeling for fasteners; finding the hooks; unlatching them. It's funny; that's how I thought of it at the time, unlatching them. I thought of the old-fashioned latches on the doors in his grandmother's house, and that conjured up the image of the quilted bed in Mary Katherine's guestroom. I imagined doing it with him in that bed, in that room. So much more erotic: A touch of danger to it, the danger of discovery. His hands slid down my sides. One-handed, he popped the fasteners on my skirt, and let it fall about my ankles. Lastly, his hands slid the slip I was wearing, and my panties, over my hips and slowly down my legs. It seemed that he went down on one knee to do so, because I felt the burr of his 'evening shadow' as his cheek touched my thigh. Then he stood up and moved, and I knew that he was standing in front of me, and that he was looking at me. I opened my eyes.

We were facing each other, with only eighteen inches, maybe two feet between us. He reached towards me with his hands and cupped his palms under my breasts, then let them slide down across my stomach. I caught them just below my navel.

"Wait!" I said. "Let me."

But he didn't let me. He slipped out of his jacket and pulled a jumper up over his head, then followed that with a sweatshirt. All that was left for me to do was unbuckle his belt, unfasten the tongue of his waistband, and pull down the zip of his trousers. I went behind him to do this, and then slid his boxer shorts over his hips as he had just done with my panties, even to going down on one knee. My eyes were just level with his erection, and as I rose to my feet, I folded one hand about it from underneath. He shivered with apprehension and I folded my other arm about him and kissed him hard on the mouth. I pulled him with me to the nearer of the two beds and lay back under him on top of the cover. Knowing it was his first time I guided his hand as he explored my own intimacy, then helped him to penetrate me. He gasped with the unexpected sensation, and I moaned back at him, feeling through him all the virginal pleasure of doing it for the first time without that first time pain.

"Slowly," I panted at him, "take your time. Come slowly."

I wanted it to last all night. Wanted the two of us to twist and writhe, like two serpents in congress, but there was no containing him. He was like some great whale; no, not a whale, a sleek shiny dolphin exploding out of the deep, and crashing back to send waves of pleasure cascading over me. I was washed in ecstasy, and when the climax came, it was as if the two of us sank through an infinity of blue, an ocean as deep as space it self.

Not even with Owen Friel, a man starved of all normal contact for fifteen years, was it like this.

It registered, briefly, that I had fucked both the Godfather and the Godson, but I had no hang up about that. This is the new age. We take what we want, and want no excuse. We need none. But this Godson surprised me. He didn't just fall asleep. He lay on his back beside me and held my hand.

"Close your eyes," he said. A favourite phrase, it seemed.

"Close your eyes, so that we can see."

"Imagine", he said, "Imagine that we can be anything we want to be; fish in the sea; giants; stars; anything!"

"Birds", I suggested.

"Birds are good," he answered, "seabirds, perhaps."

I thought of images I had seen - on video somewhere, of gannets, surfing the wind and plunging like living darts into a seething ocean. The image appealed to him, and he was quiet for awhile, as if he was a PC downloading and saving a series of pictures.

"Add some islands," he said next, "low, granite islands. Summer islands, with grassy green stretches between the grey outcrops of rocks. They must have beaches, though; white, sandy beaches with pebbly riffles of quartz gravel."

I guessed he was recalling the islands he had talked about earlier, maybe some particular island.

"How many?" I asked, and had to repeat it. "How many islands?"

"Why, seven," he answered.

"Is that all of them?" I asked yet again.

"Well," he said, "Counting the rocky islets where only the seabirds roost, there are thirteen."

Prime numbers. Seven and thirteen: 'magic' numbers. "Brilliant," I thought, although any thirteen is scary.

"Can you see them?" he asked.

It sounds naff, but I did. I had an out of body experience and soared high over a great bay dotted with islands. Here and there, black oblong shapes moved over the sun-flecked, dark-blue surface of the water. Close to some of the islands, the water was a brighter blue, and this edged into a rim of white where the sea touched the rocks and the beaches. I felt myself a part of him, and was in no way startled when the image reversed totally and I found myself looking up as he lowered himself on top of me. It was slower, gentler, this second time, and as we climaxed, I felt again that I had diffused into his persona, and as he withdrew, I shivered.

He came onto me a third time in the middle of the night, rousing me from a nervous kind of a sleep to do it urgently, like older people, out of need. Then, as I wakened with the brightness of the new morning to a room that was already too hot from the radiator, I saw him lying naked and uncovered on the bed beside me. I laid my hand on him, and his skin quivered the way the skin of a high-strung horse does. He woke instantly, the way Owen Friel did, that morning; then we made love again, for the fourth time.

Four times! Not a 'magic' number, but the next best thing; a multiple; the square of two.

Afterwards, he stood looking at his own reflection in a full-length mirror that was set on the wall facing the two beds. From where I was, I had a double image, both a full frontal – in reflection – and a rear view. I rolled over and reached for a camera. Incredibly, he never moved, and I captured in one just exactly what I had first seen, the sex still wet on him.

I never saw any man lose his inhibitions so quickly. I've said that already. When I close my eyes, I can still see him. But there was something about that double image that niggled. It bothered me. I tried to put it out of my mind. Then, just as I was on the point of falling asleep again, it came to me. Owen Friel; it had to do with the picture I had of Owen Friel. It was too two-dimensional. The image lacked depth, a second image; a reflection. Where was I, where were we, to get that?

CHAPTER THIRTEEN

THE QUESTION IS WHY?

Diary: Fifth Ruan Coll entry.
Jenny Stronnach's journal.

"Get up!"

The voice had an authority that was not there before.

"We have a dinner date."

Then he corrected himself:

"Lunch, a lunch date; in Barna; it's only three miles away. I have made coffee for you."

The coffee was black. There was no milk. I had already used all those mini tubs of half-and-half the hotel provided. Ruan was dressed. I joked about it being only the second time I had seen him dressed in a hotel room. He was too serious to appreciate it. Not serious the way he was before, there was an extra dimension to him. He had grown up. And his mission in life was still there; find the man who killed his mother. I shivered, realising it. I had seen his passion, had shared an entire night of it, and felt as if I had been to bed with a tiger. The will to kill is itself a passion, and I knew then that when he killed, it would also be as a tiger kills: savagely and unrestrained.

"You have time to shower and dress."

His voice interrupted my thoughts, and I laughed at his un-intended humour.

"God," he said, "You're beautiful. You're something special, Stronnach. You can fuck half the night – what am I talking about, the whole night – then sleep like a baby all morning, and laugh at me when I wake you. Is this the way it's supposed to be?"

I laughed at him again for his pretended innocence and made as if to pull him into the bed. I think that if I had persisted, he would have come. That would have made a five. But I had to be satisfied with the square of two, and he waited, and watched out of the window while I showered and dressed. Then I checked my cameras and selected what I might need for the day.

I don't know why I didn't ask him, who we were meeting, who it was we were to take lunch with. Something to do with the place we were to meet, perhaps. Barna! Just a village on the outskirts of Galway, beyond the edge of the city, on the coast road west: It had clearly been developed, but the extending arm of the city touched it only at fingertip, as it were. I had eaten at one of the restaurants there on a previous occasion, and it fascinated me. It had such a 'European' feel to it, old, but natural. Not like the stretch immediately to the west of the village, where a wave of late twentieth century development gave the impression that this is what the Irish would have built had they lived on the Italian Riviera. I should like to drive that road in daylight with Ruan, as we did yesterday evening. Young as he is, he seems to have a feeling for what was there before, and if I could, I would have him interpret the landscape for me. Maybe another time!

It was the pub on the corner we went into, after he parked the car in a landscaped yard at the back. Our lunch date – dates – were there before us: Ruan's Aunt Martina, and Owen Friel! I shrank back when I saw him. I swear I blushed. I felt he would know, instinctively, I had bedded Ruan, just by looking at me. He was sober this time, as he had been that first occasion we met, on the road from the prison: More than sober, rational! He put his hand on my arm, briefly, as the four of us sat into a table together.

"Hello," he said, "it's nice to meet you again."

I struggled to answer him. It was as if I could still feel the strength of his two hands under me, and I instantly wanted to fold him into me, just as I had done in the hotel room at the lake on the Shannon.

"Jesus," I thought, "this is crazy."

He took his hand away in a natural kind of a movement, and although I know I blushed, I think neither of the other two noticed. I hope they didn't. The corner of the snug we were occupying was dark, the window was small and old-fashioned, and the brightness of the day outside disguised my discomfort. But I knew then, more than ever, that what came to me in bed that morning was true. The image I had of this man was only two-dimensional. Pictures alone would not do justice to him, no matter how good the photography. Lenses would be inadequate, not unless they were fashioned from experience and polished with understanding. I would need to get a lot closer, and that would be dangerous.

Martina was sharp, hostile even. Maybe she had noticed.

"What's she doing here?" I overheard her saying to Ruan, "and how did you know we were in the area?"

Ears burning, I answered her directly myself:

"Because I was invited; because I've been drawn into this thing; because I've been made party to information that few beyond your own family and circle of friends are privy to; and because I'm not sure that any of it, or all of it, is true."

That's how I answered her. That threw down the gauntlet. That rose the three of them, literally. They were like forest pines towering over me. I remained seated.

"And because I dare ask the questions that each of you are afraid to ask. That's why I'm here, and because I like those of you I've met; so far."

They sat down again, and we were all silent.

I was the one who broke the silence.

"The question is, why?"

That's what I said.

"Why?"

Then I realised I had wet myself. Jesus! I couldn't believe it. I had peed my pants. Not seriously, but embarrassingly. I was instantly uncomfortable. Whether it was Owen Friel's hand on my arm, or the three of them rising over me, or my own temper in confronting them that caused it, I didn't know. But I withdrew with as much dignity as I could muster, excused myself, and headed for the Ladies Room. There, as I discarded the offending garment, I realised that none of them knew, and knickerless, I rejoined them.

Ruan had again taken a lead. He was explaining how he had spotted Martina's car from the window of the hotel while he was waiting for me "to shower and dress", and had recognised her passenger, then had called her on her mobile. He was quite deliberate in his choice of words, and I was only just quick enough to catch a raised eyebrow on Martina's face. She held her peace. By the time I looked at Owen Friel the moment had passed, and he was inscrutable. Ruan never paused.

"Jenny is right," he said, "the question is 'Why?' Why did my father die? And I know there is no answer to that. But why did my mother die? And why did Owen go to prison, without a defence, when it wasn't him that killed her?"

I marvelled that he could so clearly reaffirm Owen Friel's innocence. I wouldn't. But I remembered him saying, that it was when he asked Owen Friel, in prison, to tell him straight out that he had murdered his – Ruan's – mother; and that Owen Friel was not able to say that, in any words; that he, Ruan, knew he had not.

I looked back at Ruan again. He was eyeing Owen. A remorseless challenge! It was Owen that yielded. It was not a 'surrender' though. It was an explanation between equals. For a second time that day I felt uncomfortable. These men were two faces of the same sculpture; wonderfully crafted, and basalt at the core. I thought of the mirrored frontal image I had captured in the hotel room. No wonder I fancied the two of them. I looked across to Martina.

"I have the advantage of you," I thought, "I can bed both of them."

But the look that she returned spelled danger for me.

"I know that you have" it said.

CHAPTER FOURTEEN

IT'S NOT ENOUGH

What a difference a day makes! Courage can either come to you or desert you. I'm the one that should know. Twice it devastated me, when they were killed; when he was killed, and she disappeared; and I had to claw it back, morning by morning. That's the way it's done; you find explanation in the night to fashion a kind of reason with during the day. That's the way I did it. I refused to be crushed. No night was ever too black for me to fathom. I probed all with a kind-of, extra-sensory sonar, making the darkness visible, and in all those years, if I lost faith or hope at any time, only I knew it, and I mended the loss before anyone else could see my weakness. My guard never slipped. Until yesterday! That's what threw me. That maggot of an instruction from Conaghan; it was the worm in the flesh. A seemingly senseless hint that I should be in that place, at that time, and what happened? Andrew Brodie happened. That's what happened. Andrew bloody Brodie happened: Just driving along! And the same Andrew Brodie just happened to be the one, Owen Friel claimed, that shot my mother. What did I do? I ran!

Never again!

But I'm glad I came west. The night followed the day, and what a night it was! Invited back, I went; a willing novice. There will be darker nights again. This one was all light. I didn't need my mind to see on this occasion, the eyes were adequate. I don't know if she understood that. Maybe not, how could she? When I disrobed her that first time and she trembled, ever so slightly, I wondered no more why I had waited so long for that first time, and as she writhed beneath me I discovered a power within me I never knew existed. Divest of clothes, I could discover in her body the wonder even of the downy body hair on her belly, and, roused, could discover in myself the power to love. That raw, physical power! I never dreamed it would be so urgent. As urgent, almost, as the need to kill! That was something she wouldn't understand. I think only Owen Friel and I know what that feels like. Not that we had ever discussed it; it was just something I imagined. That's why I didn't need to ask him 'Why?' I knew why. How else could he get close to whatever organisation killed her, killed Frances? But I wanted to hear it, in his own words, unprompted. Even more than that, I wanted to know what part Conaghan had in all this. There was a smell about his involvement, a flavour, and it was getting stronger, but I couldn't quite get a handle on it. In any case it had to be Owen Friel first.

We cornered him in that bar, Jenny Stronnach and I. Martina ran cover for him, tried to protect him, everything except physically impose herself between us and him, but he didn't need her to do that. He was again the man I always thought him to be. The memories of a boy of seven can be suspect, but mine were true of this man, this best friend of my father's, this Godfather that he chose for me. He was like an oar of finest Ash, true in the grain, without a trace of warp, and resilient right to the end. He opened the conversation simply enough.

"I should never have doubted you. You are your father's son. You can see almost what is not there. I must hand it to you; there's not another would have seen me in Martina's car from a bedroom window."

I acknowledged the compliment with only a nod.

"We were headed for Rossaveal. I'm looking for a small boat, something that two or three could handle, I'll not find it easy to get crew, you know."

Again I nodded. Not too many would be willing to ship with a convicted murderer. In any case, anyone with any kind of experience wanted a berth on the 'big' boats, the pelagic trawlers; the money was better. So they thought. I thought differently. The right man, with the right craft, and the right gear, could take a damn fine living out of fishing around the shore. But I wondered at Owen settling for something as mundane. He finished what he started to say.

"One of the Aran men has a craft for sale, with a licence. She's handy; big enough to go off on the deep edge as well, on the fine day."

"Jesus," I thought, he's going sub-hunting!"

I didn't ask anymore. I knew now what he was about. I didn't know how, but I knew he was going to search for the seabed listening-device – I wouldn't exactly call it a microphone – or video device, that had to be on the seabed near where my father was killed. Listening devices were surely old-hat. One had drifted ashore on the Mayo coast not long after the accident, and yet another was trawled up in Galway Bay in 1986, a year afterwards. But nothing that looked like video equipment

"Martina was just obliging me with the transport."

The odd remark pulled me back out of my thoughts, back from the questions I wanted to ask him.

"They'll keep." I said to myself. Then I could hold it no longer.

"Why? Why in God's name did you let yourself go to prison, a convicted felon, for life, for murder, for the murder of my mother, when you didn't do it?"

The answer was devastatingly simple.

"Because I couldn't prove that I didn't kill her."

He hesitated just a moment, then spoke again very deliberately.

"and because I felt guilty. No matter what, I was responsible. I shouldn't have asked your mother to drive my car to Dublin to collect me."

He looked at Martina.

"If I were to ask anyone, it should have been Martina. Nothing was ever promised between us, but I always felt that we would have got it together, eventually, but that there was no rush to do so. We were comfortable together. Then the night of your father's funeral happened."

He was talking to me now.

"I was so guilty about that. I should never have let it happen."

He jumped forward into his story again.

"Do you know, the police couldn't even find the house where it happened, where we had been held prisoner, afterwards. So they said. And I couldn't search, myself, I was denied bail. It was because of that I decided to present no defence. I figured that if I couldn't follow up on the outside, I would do it from inside the prison. I was bound to be sent to the top security prison, where the likes of IRA prisoners would be sent, and I thought that sooner or later, I would learn who it was that hijacked us."

"And did you?" I interjected, but he continued as if I had said nothing.

"I suspected the IRA. Who else could it be, I thought? But I was wrong. One day, in the exercise yard, I heard that voice again, that voice that had shouted 'Shoot the fucking bitch!' and I knew at last who it was: McMenamy, Ernan McMenamy, an LRA man. He's 'respectable' now."

I could hear the parentheses in his voice, the way he spat the word 'respectable' out.

" I had already served four years when that happened, and the next four years were the most dangerous, and the most frustrating, of my entire life."

"How so?"

The suddenness of that simple question startled all of us. It was Jenny Stronnach who burst in with it. Wrapped in the past, we had reverted to considering her a stranger, and had forgotten that she was even there. But she was not one to be ignored. She startled all three of us into silence. Then, Owen Friel answered her.

"Because each of us knew who the other was, and each of us lived only to kill the other."

"And did either of you try?"

This was Jenny Stronnach again.

"We were never allowed the chance. It was as if the warders, no, the prison authorities – it had to be further up the ladder – knew exactly who we were and what was between us. But there came one day, when I was showering, and I thought I was alone. The lights went out. I knew instantly I was in danger.

Putting the lights out was their mistake; I had spent too many nights on darkened hillsides when I was growing up, and too many days in solitary because I didn't follow anybody's rules in prison, to be hampered by the dark. I needed no special submarine equipment to make the darkness visible."

"What happened?"

Jenny wanted no narrative whatsoever, only the story, instantly.

"I karate-chopped him across the throat, that's what happened. And I smashed another guy's skull on the tiles, broke three of them. He lived. So did McMenamy. Warders jumped me before I could kill him. They must have been waiting. I always knew him just by the voice, by that nasal twang of his. That's what I called him in my mind all those years, the 'Voice'. From then on it was even more distinctive, I crushed his larynx."

There were no more questions from Jenny Stronnach, or from Martina. His account of such a brutal encounter was so matter-of-fact, so off the wall, that they found it hard to reconcile with the man sitting so normally with us at a pub table.

"What happened afterwards?" I asked him.

"Solitary!" he answered. "Solitary, until they finally released McMenamy; a political arrangement. Even then, I might still have been kept in solitary if it hadn't been for Mary Katherine. She came to see me, insisted on it. She allowed them no excuse for not producing me. She persuaded me to attempt a course through the Open University. It was a heavy meeting, she could scarcely bring herself to look at me. After all I was the man convicted of killing her daughter. I don't think she would have done it if my father had not asked her to look out for me, before he died."

His narrative dried up then. When I looked at him, the tears were wet in his eyes: Thinking of his father, perhaps. Then he said something that made me doubt my conclusion.

"How, in Jesus' name, am I going to find her body?"

Abruptly, he got up from the table and went out into the sunshine. Martina half rose to go after him, but Jenny Stronnach reached out her hand and gently caught hold of her arm.

"There's something you might not know," she said. "Mary Katherine put a 'geis' on him to find your sister's body, I think he feels he can never do it."

We filed out of the bar after him. He had walked a little ways down the narrow road, towards the single pier that enclosed a small bit of a harbour, and had stopped at the wall of an old graveyard. The rusty gate was fastened only with a simple latch, but he made no attempt to go in. He leaned on the almost shoulder-high moss-covered stones. He repeated what he had just said in the bar.

"How, in Jesus' name, am I to find her body?"

Both Martina and Jenny Stronnach made moves to cross over the road to him. I reached after Jenny and held her back.

"It's time for us to go," I said.

We made our excuses and left. But as we turned away, I called out to Owen over my shoulder:

"I want to keep in touch. Let Martina know where you can be reached. I can phone her."

Then, we were gone.

We stopped off at her hotel in Salthill, just on the edge of Galway City, to the west, to check out. The night was already a memory, but I followed her up to her room, and stood while she packed her case, clearing drawers, twisting clothes hangers deftly out of dresses and skirts and blouses. The blouses were more shirts than blouses, I noticed, and the packing included several pairs of jeans which she took, folded, from one of the drawers. She was nearly finished, when she held up a pair of panties.

"You'll excuse me," she said, "I've no knickers on."

It was like a trigger to me: An instantaneous fuse. My arousal was total. I scattered the packed case out of the way and tumbled her back on the bed, heedless of her protestations. Her skirt had risen up her thighs, and I fumbled at my flies. Eventually she yielded to me, and I made love to her there again on top of the bed, for the fifth time in twenty-four hours, and she moaned with the pleasure of it. Afterwards she murmured that two times two would have been enough, and I didn't know what she was talking about.

She fell asleep in the car on the run to Dublin, waking only once to mutter:

"You must tell him to close his eyes. That's what he has to do, close his eyes. Then he will be able to see."

With that, she fell back asleep again, and I didn't know what that was about either.

CHAPTER FIFTEEN

CONAGHAN, OK; BUT WHAT ABOUT BRENNAN?

Fuck Conaghan. That's all I could think of on the run to Dublin. Fuck him. Why couldn't he come clean and tell me all at once. I still hadn't heard his own second tape – he didn't afford me a chance to talk to him, not really, when I got back from Donegal – and, at this stage, I was ready to believe he could even have another. Fuck him. That was another car passed. That's the way I was driving; shoeing on when I thought the road was clear – I mean no cops with hairdryers – slowing to the sixty mile speed limit when I thought there might be, and gunning the motor every time I needed to overtake. The miles dropped behind. Jenny Stronnach slept through it all, except for that one time she stirred and muttered,

"You must tell him to close his eyes. Then he will be able to see."

What did she mean by that, I wondered? I puzzled away at it for a while, but could find nothing rational in it, and concentrated again on my driving. The car ahead was half American in styling, broad and boxy, that dark, dark wine colour, one of the big Volvos. Some businessman driving it.

"Fuck you," I said for no particular reason, "and your fucking big Volvo," and I floored the accelerator.

I nearly went over the top of him. I hadn't realised I had such a pick-up in my own car, one of the older Renaults, and I only just avoided ramming him from behind.

"And fuck Conaghan as well."

It was an understatement to say I was mad. All I wanted was the truth, and I felt I was getting the run-around. It was never like this. Is this what sex does for you, I wondered? For all the fuck-up, life had been like a fine wool polo; it fitted me. All I needed were the shades, and the wheels. Then something pulled a thread in it and it all started to unravel. That something was the occasion, just a couple of weeks ago now, when Conaghan told me Owen Friel was to get early release. Before that, I was clean cut, well spoken. Now I fucked like a Dublin comedian. I thought myself I might have cooled down by the time I got to the city, to Dublin, but I was even less in control than I realised. Somehow I was pumping pure testosterone. I ran three red lights in a row on the outskirts of the city, and got away with it. Others didn't. Three cars whacked each other at one of the crossings, two at another. If there was a devil, he was sitting on my shoulder, and he laughed all the way. Jenny Stronnach slept through it all, but the snooze ended when I slammed the brakes on in the alleyway at the back of the Paper.

"Out!" I ordered her, "Out! We're here." And I bundled her out of the car and in through the works door.

We almost collided with Doyle – the 'reliable' – in the constriction where the clock-cards were racked. I don't know why he was leaving just at that moment; I would have expected him to be in the newsroom. In the delay of untangling ourselves, I thought on the spur of the moment to ask him about Conaghan.

"Is there something I don't know about O'C?" I asked him. "Is there any reason he might have it in for the LRA?"

"Jesus!" Doyle said to me. "Jesus, Where have you been? How long have you been with us? Of course, you're only just a year with the paper. How could you know?"

He looked at me as if I had only just had my nappy changed.

"His son was killed in a bomb explosion, and his wife lost a leg. Did you not know?"

He saw the next question in my eye.

"About twelve, no, maybe only eleven years ago; at Christmas! The Punt was strong at the time. Things were supposed to be quiet, safe! Fleets of buses went north for the shopping."

He anticipated my next query.

"No one admitted responsibility, but it was thought to be the LRA. Andrew Brodie had been arrested in the South. He was caught at a checkpoint with detonators in the car. Got four years, I think. Some reckoned it a retaliation. The bomb, I mean."

His final look said all that needed to be said; about his failure to comprehend my ignorance; and about my feeling of stupidity. That knocked the tost out of my testosterone. Jenny Stronnach came to my rescue; she tugged at my elbow.

"We have someone to see;" she said, "let's do it."

It was as if I was a kid's toy, one of those friction-drive cars that had been momentarily lifted off the floor, then set down again. The built up energy kicked in again and I stormed down the newsroom like some cyclone, sucking Jenny Stronnach after me in my wake.

The newsroom was a new affair, all high-tech and computer screens, but essentially laid out on traditional lines. A great L-shaped open plan room, only two glass-panelled offices obtruded, midway along the outside wall, on the shared space. One was the News editor's, the other was Conaghan's. The area in front of Conaghan's was clear, a kind of a no-man's land between the reporters and the sub-editors. This was where the nightly 'conference' happened, where the lead stories and the daily layout of the paper were decided upon. And when Conaghan and his principal editors were in conference, no one disturbed them.

I swept straight through them, with Stronnach behind me picking her way over the debris as it were, and right in the open door of Conaghan's office. Then the two of us stood there, waiting. It was a direct challenge that Conaghan couldn't ignore, and as it was he who had to move, we had the advantage of him. That was not how the newsroom saw it. Work stopped. Reporters, subs, and editors alike clearly anticipated a fireworks display of Desert Storm proportions. They weren't disappointed.

Conaghan had the reputation of being cool under fire – I guess that was why he was Editor – and had the skill to lose it when he needed to. I had youth and all that inexperience on my side, so I got my retaliation in first. That was one of the main lessons I learnt in boarding school.

"Never play silly buggers with me," I said to him, "I'm too fucking dangerous."

To his credit, I don't think he was, but it was only in the argument that I realised it, and I hadn't reached that realisation just yet. He had closed the door of the office behind him, so to the surreptitiously eager onlookers the show must have looked like one of those silent-film cartoon dogfights. You know, where heads, arms and feet - to say nothing of sticks, bats and cudgels - appear momentarily from a cloud of dust, only to disappear again in the melee. Not that the office was soundproofed. No one can have been in any doubt as to what I wanted: A complete expose and re-investigation of the Frances Coll 'murder', and Owen Friel's conviction. A crusading campaign; and hell mend the consequences! I wanted the full backing of the Paper, and no more being fucked around. I used worse language than that. There were words that I barely knew the meaning of, because I had never used them. I deployed all of them that night, in their exactitude.

At one stage it became so heated, arms being waved, fists brandished, seemingly no resolution possible, that I stopped, very deliberately opened the door and ushered Jenny Stronnach out of the office.

"You will excuse us." I said, then pushed her out and closed the door behind her. The row resumed.

It took another five minutes, then we quietened. Five minutes more and we shook hands. I glanced briefly out of the office, and thought them almost on the verge of applause, but the heads dropped as soon as they realised I was looking at them. I walked out then, down the newsroom and caught up with Jenny who was waiting just outside the door. Taking her arm, we started down the stairs.

"Well?" she asked, did you get it?"

"I did." I answered.

"How?" she asked.

"I told him I'd fucking shoot him." I replied.

She knew I'd meant it. As he did.

She laughed; a nervous, relieved kind of a laugh.

Just then the print room Production Manager came flying round the landing and up the stairs three at a time.

"What the fuck is going on, then? Have they all fucking died? Don't they know we have a paper to get out?"

For a second time that evening we had to untangle ourselves and, as we were doing so, Jenny asked:

"What about Brennan? Did you remember to ask him about Brennan?"

"Jesus!" I said, "I forgot about Brennan. Fuck."

Then I turned on the instant and marched back into the newsroom again.

The place was abuzz, but it wasn't work. Conaghan still hadn't left his office, and I caught him with his hand on the doorknob. He opened the door ahead of me; and anticipating my question; said quietly:

"It's Brennan, isn't it? You want to know about Brennan! I'll tell you tomorrow. Be in my office in the morning; about eleven o'clock; I'll be in; we'll work out the details. Now fuck off, I've a paper to get out."

That satisfied me. I slept in my own bed that night. I was drained.

CHAPTER SIXTEEN

GIRL'S NIGHT IN / THE WAITING

Jenny Stronnach / Ruan Coll.

Just like that! Good night! That's all? Then he walks away. No hug! Not a cuddle! Kissless! Bloody useless! Just when a girl thought…..

What did a girl think? He was a man? Yes, I suppose so. No, I know so. That's what makes it hard. He is a man. Maybe young, maybe inexperienced – but he learns fast. God, what a night and a day! No wonder I slept in the car; I was never so exhausted. He makes me, no, that's not right, because I don't know if it will ever happen again; he made me feel as if he wanted me. It almost seemed as if he wanted to consume me. No one ever made me feel like that, not even Owen Friel. That was weird. Nothing ever came over me like that. I wanted him so much. But, God, what a body! Like coiled super-springs under a covering of flesh. Then, when he laid his hand on me, and I peed myself! What have I come to? Serves me right for fucking two men.

*** *** ***

The morning was more difficult than I thought it would be. Levelling with people, accepting them, on a one-to-one basis, meant losing control. I never realised that would be the price. Somehow I thought I would be the captain of my destiny, but it doesn't happen like that. It didn't for my father or my mother; why did I expect it would happen for me? I never thought it would be so painful to crack open the crab-like carapace I had so deliberately formed around me. I accepted Doyle as part of the team. As Conaghan said, "He was reliable." He would be the anchorman, always at base, answering to the Chief. Jenny – I had been careless earlier, had not adequately acknowledged her, and had been kicked on the shin for it – Jenny was given a free hand on the photographs.

"Whatever she comes up with. Her own, or from the archives!"

That's what Conaghan said.

I was uncomfortable right away. Not that I felt it wrong to give her photographic control, but I was suddenly conscious of an image of her aiming a camera from the bridge over the Shannon the morning Owen Friel was released from prison.

"Jesus" I thought, "she never would, would she? I mean the two of us were bollock naked; well all but."

But I got a grip of myself.

"If this is what it takes to get at the truth of what happened, and find my mother's body, so be it. I'll wear it. And with luck I'll get the chance to come face to face with the bastards that did it; the one that called the shot, and the one that fired it."

I looked across at Jenny, and had no idea what it was that she saw, but as we were leaving she unexpectedly said to me: "That's it then. Partners! We're buddies. More than buddies. We're an item. Remember it. And I'm not including Doyle in."

I looked at her. Then Conaghan called me back; handed me a tape.

"You might like to listen to this."

"What is it?" I asked. "Who's on it?"

"Owen Friel" he said.

"A second tape?" I asked.

"It is." he said.

"I kind-of figured you might have another tape," I said, "but I've heard his story. He told me himself."

"Not like this, you haven't," Conaghan said, "I recorded this myself the night he was arrested."

"Jesus!" I said. "How?" I said.

"I got a ladder," he said, "and climbed into the yard at the back of the police station. Then I put the ladder up to the window of the cell. There is a hell of a fall to the rere. You can see that from the road."

I nodded. He continued.

"I taped over the window, it was tiny, and I put my elbow to it. I fed the lead of the mike in through the hole and recorded him from the ladder. I took the broken glass, and the tape it was stuck to, away with me. I threw them in the Ballinahown River."

"Jesus," I said, " that's obstructing justice. You could be jailed!"

"Yes," he said, "that's why I never used it."

"You still could be," I said, "they'd fucking hang you."

I was enjoying this: The sheer outrageousness of it. I knew, then, we would succeed, in whatever it was we were trying to do. I thought of the two men who were the targets of our vengeance, of our vindictiveness, and I shivered. Once terrorists and vilified, now politicians and feted; regarded even as statesmen; they were already dead men walking.

I turned for the door again.

"Play it," Conaghan called after me, "it's what he said at the time, before O'Hara beat the shit out of him. Nobody except me has ever heard this account of what happened."

"What was it?" Jenny Stronnach asked when I caught up with her.

"Nothing!" I answered her, but I knew she didn't believe me.

* * *   * * *   * * *

This wine isn't working. I should be drunk – or asleep, by now. But I'm not. I'm neither pissed nor sober, and definitely not asleep. Why is that? I know I slept in the car, but I needed to. If I hadn't, I'd have screwed him all the way to Dublin. But he walked away without even a goodnight. I've written that already, haven't I? Have to move on. This eating alone is crap. Shell pasta with packet sauce is no substitute for red meat, even if it is garlic sauce. And the other chair is empty. There's no body in it; no knees under the table to knock against my knees; to insinuate themselves between my legs; no hands to reach over to mine, to pick pasta shells carelessly off my plate; no breath breathing hot on me across the table.

Jesus, I hope nobody ever reads this; they'll think I've lost it. I only hope I haven't lost him. He's something special. I don't think I ever met anybody quite like him. To have lost both his parents, in the way that he did, and still to be a human being! And he is that: A real person! I know these are new times, and it's supposed to be easy now for us women, but it's not. It's fucking difficult. It's a battle every day, with nothing much at the end of it, most days, except to walk out of the darkroom, and put a saucepan of water on the gas to cook some pasta. Fuck pasta. I want meat. Big Charollais steaks, two of them, and the man and the trimmings to go with them. And he's the candidate. He's a bit raw yet. Not much more than a sapling that has cracked its way out of the rock, and I can be both the sun and the rain for him. But what does he see? Ernan fucking McMenamy! Him, and revenge! And the bitch of it is, I can't blame him.

* * *   * * *   * * *

It was worth listening to, that tape of Conaghan's. Just for one thing, and I nearly didn't hear it. I was so taken with the sound of Owen's voice, with the strength of the anger in it, that I almost missed it. I was living the experience with him; how he crashed in desperation through the curtained window and tumbled, unexpectedly, down a rusty galvanised iron roof. I was sick with him all over again in his despair at his failure to save my mother, and ran heedlessly with him when he landed half on his feet and raced off blindly into the darkness. But I felt also how his natural instinct for making his way through wild countryside in the dark of night reasserted itself, and rotated my head upwards, as he did, to check the night sky. Then locating the 'Plough', and from it, the North Star, he ran on doggedly into the nor'ard.

"Gotcha!" I said to myself, then I remembered the same expression and the nastily triumphant way it was uttered on that other tape that was sent only a few weeks previously to Conaghan, and I regretted saying it.

"All the same, now I know how to start looking," I thought. "We just need to get Owen Friel to remember where it was that he emerged on the main road, and we backtrack to the southward from there."

I was disappointed the following day, and on the next day again, when Conaghan wasn't there. I had no one to tell my 'discovery' to. Doyle, I felt, would not understand. Jenny Stronnach was searching the archives for photographs from the time of the accident, from the time of the trial also. There were plenty from both occasions. Those from the time of the accident pictured the ambulance and the shocked crowds on the pier head as the 'Ocean Voyager' came to shore. One particularly poignant one, seemingly taken from the roof of the Auction Hall, caught a moment when one of the stretcher-bearers stumbled and went down on one knee on the gangplank. Those nearest the gangplank had recoiled momentarily and it looked as if the bearers and their burden had been dropped in the middle of the crowd, and what was captured was the initial ripple. On a different level, the picture portrayed a sacred thing, with the stretcher-bearer genuflecting as he came sacredly ashore. When Jenny Stronnach showed it to me, it was too much for me, and I left them, her and Doyle, and went across the road to the pub.

* * *   * * *   * * *

That did it all right, the hot chocolate and the brandy! How long have I been asleep? It feels like hours. But I'm still up. I need to go to bed.

But why can't I? Something's bothering me. Something I did? Can't be. I haven't that much conscience. Something I said? Surely not! A dream; it must have been a dream. Maybe all this is just a dream, and if I can only go to sleep again, I'll wake up in the morning and it won't even be a memory. But it's not, is it? It's real. A nightmare! And it's all true. An ordinary man clawed his way from practically nothing to a pinnacle of achievement; scarcely more than thirty, he took delivery of the most powerful trawler afloat, and then, "in the twinkling of an eye", had his whole life snatched from him. It would have been better, almost, if he had never been. Then, a rapacious destiny swallowed up his widow. And I get involved with his son.

It's coming back to me now; something I said to Ruan in the car on the journey back from Galway. It had something to do with a thing he had said earlier to me. That's it. "Close your eyes" he said to me, and I did. I closed them, and as he talked, I could see all the things he was talking about. Then, I could see even more; seabirds with outstretched wings, stationary almost in the air, held there by the strength of the ocean breeze. And in the car, when I was asleep and dreaming of everything that happened after he came across from Armagh and took me to dinner, it came to me that all Owen Friel needed to do was close his eyes in the same way. Our memory is a function of the visual cortex, and Owen Friel's memories must be burnt in as if with a laser: CDs of living flesh. All we need is a read head. Now I know what it was I said to him in the car:

"You must tell him to close his eyes. That's what he has to do, close his eyes. Then he will be able to see."

I must write this down so that I will be sure to tell Ruan. Now I can go to sleep.

*** *** ***

I got bloody picked up, in the pub. What else would you call it? They – there were two of them – they picked me up just by walking over and introducing themselves to me. Alice LaCombre, and Robert. She spelt it out for me. She didn't say whether Robert was her husband or her brother, or indeed if he was anything at all to her. They were of an age with my parents, if my parents had lived. They looked good. Too good for where they said they hailed from: Honea Path, Southern Carolina. It sounded rural, Southern. They neither looked nor walked rural. For that matter, they didn't talk 'country'. I don't really know what people from the South sound like, but these two sounded just 'American'. Even their shoes looked wrong, they were city wear. Nevertheless, I took them to be what they appeared to be: Tourists who had just wandered in off the street.

I know I was vulnerable. The photographs of my father's body being carried ashore had pierced the mental carapace I wore always, and I needed little urging to spill the whole story. It was all the easier for them being strangers. They were beyond merely sympathetic, they cushioned every word from me, and when they asked a question, they asked it carefully, as if they wished not to hurt me further.

"A submarine," she asked when I came to that part of the story, "What kind of a submarine?"

And when I replied that it was probably a nuclear submarine, she asked:

"How would you know? Did anyone photograph it?"

I had no answer to that and she let it pass, but when I mentioned the underwater video recording, she was again quick to ask what exactly the tape showed and if I had seen it myself. It's funny, but I don't remember him asking any question, and yet I'm certain he did. Spooky! How much more of the story I told them is anybody's guess, because Jenny Stronnach came into the pub in the middle of the telling and intruded herself into the company, and that constrained me. But afterwards I remembered how interested they had been in the topic of the submarine and of the videotape, and they asked particularly about Killybegs. Jenny's interruption had effectively ended the narrative, and they excused themselves shortly afterwards and left. I had a distinct feeling we would see them again.

"I was concerned for you." Jenny said.

When I told her how they came on to me, as it were, she insisted on getting the full story.

"Jesus, Ruan," she said, "You need to be more careful. You don't know who they might be. I'm in this with you one hundred per cent, depend on it, but for Jesus' sake be careful. This story is going to rattle a lot of boxes that certain people would prefer left undisturbed. This is dangerous, and not just for you. We're all of us involved, even Conaghan; maybe especially Conaghan."

"Fuck Conaghan" I thought, but I didn't really mean it. I was frustrated. I felt impotent again. So I let it out.

"Conaghan, Where is Conaghan in any case?" I asked. We can't commit to going ahead or to a deadline without him. I know it's been only three days since he said he would, but it has already seemed like three weeks of waiting."

I grabbed her arm.

"I can't wait anymore. Now that it's started, I only want it to be finished, I don't care what bodies we leave after us, or whose blood gets spilled, I just want to get to the far side of it."

"But you want to find your mother, don't you?" she asked me, and the bitterness of my own reply shocked even myself:

"I don't believe she can be found, not really. If we're lucky we will find out for sure who killed her, and I will kill him. That's all we can hope for. In any case it's Owen Friel's job to find her body. He was the one Mary Katherine put the geis on."

I was still holding onto her arm. Suddenly she strained to get clear.

"Look!" she said. "Do you see? The CCTV, the security camera! We can check out who they were."

She pulled free of me and went to talk to the barman. Just then someone, a customer, came in through the door, and as it opened I caught a glimpse of Conaghan in the street outside. He was accompanied by a rather elegant-looking woman. I jumped for the door and was just in time to see them enter the Newspaper's offices.

"Stronnach," I shouted over my shoulder, "Conaghan's back!" and I raced across the street.

It was all of ten minutes before Jenny made it back to the newsroom, by which time I was earnestly in conversation with Conaghan, trying to impress on him how do-able it should be to get Owen Friel to track to the southward from where he struck the main road. She was just in time to hear the end of my argument, and Conaghan's answer that the trouble was, Owen Friel had no memory of where he emerged on the main road that night. The elegant-looking lady was out in the newsroom itself, talking to Doyle and some of the other reporters, and Conaghan's eyes were focused steadily on her through the glass wall of his office. I turned to look at her myself, wondering who she was. Jenny Stronnach had answered Conaghan, but I wasn't really paying attention until, suddenly, the familiarity of the phrase echoed in my memory:

"If we get him to close his eyes, then he will be able to see."

She said other things; about memory, and the visual cortex; and then something more:

"It's a way of making the darkness visible again."

Just then the elegant lady moved in our direction and I suddenly realised who she was. I didn't need Conaghan to make the introduction.

"I'm pleased to meet you, Mrs Conaghan." I said.

"Ruan, isn't it?" she answered and laid her hand on my arm. "Yes, it has to be Ruan. I remember your father."

She hesitated.

"And your mother; especially your mother. Do you think you will find her?"

I had no answer for her.

In the embarrassed silence that followed, Conaghan reached forward and took the videocassette that Jenny Stronnach was holding, almost absent-mindedly, in her hand.

"I presume this is for me," he said, and slotted it into a VCR. When the image resolved itself, it was clear that the tape was from the CCTV security camera in the pub over the road. He fast-forwarded the tape until the next customer coming into the bar could clearly be identified as myself. Then the tape picked up the two Americans. He hit the pause button and peered at the screen for several seconds. Then he looked at Mrs Conaghan, who was, herself, staring quite intently at the screen.

"What do you think?" he asked her, "what would they have looked like sixteen years ago?"

"Not him," she answered. "Her! She called herself Alice then, Alice LaCombre. I met her in the hotel in Donegal Town. It was the fortnight after Owen Friel was arrested, before they took him away to Dublin. She talked to all the media people, but never really said who she was or what she was doing there."

I distinctly saw Jenny Stronnach shiver, and felt the hair on the back of my own neck prickle.

Mrs Conaghan continued.

"But she was too obvious, too good-looking. Of course we talked to her, but she had a companion who never said very much. I thought he was the real researcher. She just asked the questions."

"Jesus!" I said.

Conaghan then called Doyle into the office, and asked his wife to excuse him for a few minutes.

"We have a few things to sort out," he told her, "and it's best that we keep you out of it."

"I'll wait for you downstairs in the reading room," she said, and she walked across the newsroom towards the stairs with that graceful step of hers.

"Now," said Conaghan as he turned to face Jenny Stronnach, "Explain this eyes closed thing again to me. Maybe you've got something."

When she had finished explaining it a second time, Doyle commented that it would be just like turning a light-switch on again.

"Not quite," she answered, "more a question of recreating the ambience of that night; the terror; the darkness; the detail. It's all there to be rediscovered, you know. In his mind."

"But it was years ago," said Doyle.

"Yes," she replied, "fifteen or sixteen years. The bloody cosmic scientists have detected the echo of the 'Big Bang', fifteen billion years on. All we have to go back is fifteen lousy years. Don't you think we can do it?"

She turned and looked to me for support. I nodded. What else could I do?

Afterwards, when he had himself left, I said to Doyle:

"Doesn't she move gracefully for a ……" and hesitated, searching for the correct word to use.

"Cripple! That's the word you're reaching for." It was Jenny Stronnach who said it. "That's the word alright, but it's not politically correct to use it anymore."

I nodded again in agreement but kept my final thought to myself:

"The bastards can maim us, and we're not even allowed to say that we have been maimed!"

CHAPTER SEVENTEEN

RECOVERED MEMORIES, ONE

The trouble was, nobody asked Owen Friel whether he would be an eyes-closed guinea pig for us or not. In fact, we hadn't even asked for his co-operation in the planned series. I had so overwhelmed Conaghan's professional prudence that he simply hadn't questioned me on it. The fact was, we hadn't got his permission, and I said nothing. Conaghan wanted me to go to Derry. He assigned me to cover the 'Saville Inquiry':

"For the moment," he said. "In two or three weeks, McMenamy will appear before it. I don't know the exact date, yet."

"Jesus," I said, "how do you know these things?"

"Sources!" he answered. "Mind," he continued, "That's not public knowledge yet. Keep it to yourself. Tell nobody, not even Owen Friel." He was silent a moment. "Especially not Owen Friel. There's no knowing what he might do. I'll tell you when you can tell him. In good time."

That was when I almost told him we hadn't got Owen Friel's agreement to anything yet; but I didn't.

The 'Saville Inquiry' into the events in 'Londonderry', on what has gone into the history of infamy as 'Bloody Sunday', had been running in public session since April 2000. The bare facts, filmed and documented in the world's press at the time in 1972, were incontrovertible: Thirteen unarmed civilians were shot dead by soldiers of the British Army, by the Paras, on the streets of Derry on a Sunday afternoon in 1972. A fourteenth died later from gunshot wounds. An earlier Inquiry, the Widgery Inquiry, had exonerated the Army, and cast the slur of terrorism on the innocent victims. No other event in the sorry list of atrocities and political blunders in Northern

Ireland did so much to trigger the real IRA terror, which was still to come. Cavalcades of cars travelled from all over County Donegal into Derry on the Sunday morning of the mass funeral at St. Mary's Church in the Creggan. I have heard my grandfather, Stephen, talk of the grim, repressed anger that under-laid the communal grief on that grey morning.

The Terror followed. Sure, it was called only 'The Troubles', but for those who became the victims, the 'collateral damage' of this bloody, sectarian conflict, I have no doubt about what it really was. It was evil, and it corrupted everyone it touched.

Owen Friel knew more about the new Inquiry than I did. I caught up with him on the quay in Killybegs. There was space about the 'Blackrock' pier where crew could work at gear, and I found him there, on his own, struggling to ready a newly bought net for sea. When I told him what had me north, he muttered "Bloody right!" and kept on at whatever he was doing. After a while, he said, "Hold this." and reached me a handful of netting. I threaded my fingers through a half a dozen of meshes and strained backwards while he mended on a 'pocket' to hold a catch sensor.

"Bloody right!" he said again as he tied off and snipped the twine, having finished the job. He folded away a pocket knife, and threw the almost empty net needle towards a small pile of filled needles lying nearby. "I was there, you know, I was at the funeral in the Creggan, with my father! Your father was there too, and your grandfather, Stephen. We huddled in against the wall of the church, but there was no warmth in that graveyard that morning. I guess McMenamy was there as well. I wonder will he give evidence to the Inquiry?"

When I made no reply, he stood and looked at me. I just let myself look stupid, as if I knew nothing.

"He hasn't appeared at it yet," Owen Friel continued. "I've been following it since it started. Since before it started for that matter. I had nothing much else to do, you know; not where I was. I think it's only right. Whether Saville is the right man remains to be seen."

Lord Saville was the Law Lord that was picked to head up the new Inquiry that was bargained out as part of the 'Good Friday' agreement, a tentative peace settlement between the disputing factions in 'The North'. Brokered by the British and the Irish Governments, it attempted to create a solution to a war that was fought by proxy. When it came down to it, none of the many different factions involved gave a shite who they maimed, or killed. It didn't seem to matter whether the victims were 'their own' people or not, the atrocity could always be laid at the door of the 'other' side. If it happened to be one of the others, that was just a bonus. And since the 'Peace Process' started, each faction seemed simply to scale down its operation to one of intimidation directed against its own particular community. So called 'punishment beatings' escalated again in frequency and barbarity.

I said as much to Owen Friel.

"But the Saville Inquiry chunters on." I added, " maybe it will deliver some good."

"Maybe, indeed," he assented, "but hardly justice."

That was when I broached what we were really about, Conaghan, Jenny Stronnach and I: To achieve justice and vindication for Owen, and my mother – because she was tainted by all that had happened.

"We intend re-opening the whole issue in a series of articles, and we need your co-operation."

He was taken aback.

"What about revenge?" he said. "Do you not still want to kill the bastards?"

"That, too," I answered him, "and to find her body, but I want her vindicated as well, and that's going to be much harder."

He was silent a long time; then he walked away leaving net and needles lying on the quay.

I was ahead of him on the pier the following morning. He came late. It was almost ten o'clock by the time I saw him walking along the shore road. I was finishing a cup of coffee from a flask I had taken with me. I had already stretched out the headline of the net. Several bags of trawl floats, and a bunch of tyings, were lying nearby, and I figured that lashing on the floats was the next job to be done.

"You have your father in you," he growled, "that's clear. He could never stand around."

Then he surprised me.

"Did you know I did a course in The Open University?" he asked. "Got it too."

I let him talk on.

"I took English Literature, and Irish History from 200 BC to the coming of the Normans."

"Why not later?" I asked him, "I mean, a later period of Irish History."

"At the creek of Baginbun, Ireland was lost and won!" he quoted at me. "Because it's too painful, I suppose. After that, there was too much betrayal."

He paused a moment, thinking, then continued.

"I suppose that's what history is all about, in every age: greed and betrayal. Betrayal and greed! A hunger for power! Territory as well. Isn't that what took the Fir Bolg north from Connaught into Ulster, and the sons of Niall of the Nine Hostages along with them; Conal and Eoghain; and the territories they occupied are named for them: Tir Chonail and Tir Eoghain: Donegal and Tyrone. And that was seven hundred years before the Normans even thought to come to Ireland.

It's the same battle they are fighting today. Then, the Fir Bolg, the 'Irishmen', pushed the Ulstermen east of the Bann, and finally into the sea. They wanted control, territory, power; and they wanted it all."

He paused for effect.

"Isn't that just what this crowd want? Power and money, and the other crowd to be pushed into the sea?"

The question in his final remark sought no answer. He had his own answer long since calculated out, and he added the final codicil.

"The trouble is, anybody they don't like is 'the other crowd'. That's why I am opposed to them."

As a statement of principle, it couldn't be clearer, but I thought to clarify something even further.

"What about this quest, this toraidheacht" – I used an Irish word – "to catch up with Brodie and McMenamy?"

"That's easy," he answered, that's personal. That's just revenge."

I didn't agree with everything he said, but it was close to my own viewpoint.

We spent the rest of the day like that, disputing with one another, and all the time working on the gear. My office-soft hands reddened into blisters, and the number of them and the size of them seemed to grow exponentially with each passing hour. Sometimes we faced each other, marrying two ropes together and straining backwards to check measurements; at other times we worked in tandem, as it were, one behind the other, lacing floats onto a headline or pieces of chain onto a foot-rope – the ground-line of a net. It's a wonder only that I didn't get blisters on my vocal chords as well, I talked so much.

It's a funny thing, the English write books about obscure events in history, and this gives any number of critics – professional and armchair alike – the opportunity to display their own prejudices and erudition in critiques and letters to literary journals.

The Irish discourse about such things in ordinary conversation.

That is the way it was with Owen Friel and myself for the entire length of that day. At times he put me on the spot to be the defender of Irish Nationalism, speaking for the likes of those we were determined to wreak vengeance on. At another time he had me defending the Unionists and their convoluted sense of loyalty to the British Crown. We even speculated as to how and on what occasion Dervorgilla, the wife of the twelfth century chieftain, Tiernan O'Rourke, first met and fell for Diarmuid McMurrough, King of Leinster. It seemed relevant, because it was McMurrough who first invited the Normans into Ireland, cementing the new alliance with the marriage of his daughter, Aoife, to the victorious conqueror, Strongbow, Earl of Pembroke. It was the enmity between O'Rourke and McMurrough that pushed McMurrough into doing what he did, and here, in 2001, eight hundred years later, we were watching the end game.

That was how that second day went. At times it was almost a father – son thing, and I warmed at the closeness of it. Other times, I remembered bitterly that it was his actions that led my mother to her death, and I hated him for it. Gone midday, I suggested a break for lunch. It seemed almost every pub in the town did bar meals, but he wasn't for it. I think perhaps he wasn't comfortable with going into those kind of sociable places where he was so well known, and we worked on. Our energy levels dropped, and my knees trembled as if I had walked on the 'hungry grass' - an Irish country explanation for the phenomenon of a low blood-sugar level - but neither of us would yield to the other. We had that stubbornness that foremen, through all of history, exploited in labouring men. Eventually, though, he conceded, and we went in on board his newly acquired vessel.

I had not seen it the previous day; it must have been moored outside one of the larger pelagic vessels. Now that it was tied alongside, I could appreciate how it might suit his needs. It was well laid out, and small enough to be operated with a minimal crew. And still, it looked to have power enough to go off on the deep edge. As he stepped off the ladder on to the deck, he dropped a baited hand line over the side, then led the way into the deckhouse and busied himself making some rough ham sandwiches, two rounds a man. Curious, I asked him what he hoped to catch alongside the pier.

"A conger," he answered, "for bait for a few pots. I want a lobster. For Martina!"

I looked at him. He nodded. I laughed softly at him, but not too loud. His next utterance caught me completely by surprise:

"Do you know how to catch an eel?" he asked me, "I mean, catch hold of an eel."

"A conger, you mean?" I asked him. "Of course. With a thumb and forefinger. Gripped tight, behind the gills."

"No," he said, " a river eel, or an eel along the shore. You need a handful of grit. Even sand will do."

He continued:

"That's what we need for McMenamy!"

"Jesus!" I said, and fucked at myself under my breath. This was the opening I was waiting for and I nearly fluffed it.

"Yes," I said, "he is a fucking eel, a poisonous fucking snake of an eel."

I marvelled at how foul spoken I had become.

"That's why we have to find where you and my mother were taken. That's why we have to give Jenny Stronnach's 'close your eyes' theory a go. We haven't much time, you know."

Then, I let the cat out of the bag.

"He's to appear before the Saville Inquiry. In two or three weeks time."

It was like a nuclear explosion.

"The fuck you say!"

He reached across the cabin table and grabbed my two arms and looked long and hard at me. And just as I had known, when I asked him that time in prison had he killed my mother, that his answered 'no' was the truth; he knew then that what I had just told him was also the truth.

"Jesus fucking Christ!" he blasphemed. "Whatever it takes," he said, I'll do whatever it takes."

The drama didn't end there. As his head appeared above the guard-rail at the edge of the quay when we were climbing back onto the pier, he stopped suddenly on the rungs above me, then reversed rapidly down again.

"You go ahead of me," he said, "and describe for me the blonde woman over beyond on the shore road."

I climbed the ladder myself and looked across the inner harbour.

"Jesus!" I was startled myself. I called down the ladder: "I know who it is. She bloody picked me up in Dublin. Some American! Alice LaCombre, she called herself."

"Not American!" he called back up to me, but he would tell me nothing more, and he stayed down on board until she had cleared.

I stopped in the hotel again that night, as I had done the previous evening, and left the door unlocked, hoping that Jenny Stronnach might try it, and, finding it on the latch, might think to come in. I had no idea where she was. I had left her with Martina the first day, and had deliberately booked us into the hotel, in separate rooms. I didn't want the hassle of explaining to Mary Katherine what we were up to with Owen Friel; her approach would have been more direct. But as I lay there trying to sleep, my back arched with the hunger in my gut for Jenny Stronnach's body, and I wished I had booked only the one room.

When finally I fell asleep, I dreamed that Alice LaCombre twisted the door handle and came towards me in the dark; and when I woke in the morning, I had no way of knowing if it were true or not.

CHAPTER EIGHTEEN

RECOVERED MEMORIES, TWO

Diary entry, Killybegs; April sometime, 2001.
Jenny Stronnach's journal.

Now why did I write that? It's not April anytime. It's the first of May for Christ's sake. Mayday! I could have been skimming a spring this morning, or up to some other witchcraft. This is the day for it. But what was I doing? Calling on people I don't know from Adam; searching for old photographs for Christ's sake; and me a photographer! What do I want with other people's snaps?

This morning, I didn't really want to be in Donegal anymore. I no longer felt sure of who I was and what I was doing here. It wasn't that I was not well received anywhere we went. It was more a feeling that there was too much courtesy extended to us. It masked the genuine hospitality that seemed to be a natural part of the people that we met. At times, I wondered if it had to do with Martina accompanying me. Mostly, I put it down to the errand we were engaged on: trying to track down photographs from sixteen years ago. Not just any photos, pictures of a disaster. For some, a Mrs Maguire and a Nancy Corrigan, and I think, one other, it was particularly harrowing; they had each lost a loved one at sea. But if it pained them, they seemed all the more solicitous to help us, and they bared whole albums to us. I felt an intruder, false.

I think I was right in feeling it had to do with Martina; rather, it had to do with Martina's long dead and disappeared sister, Frances, as much as with the terrible death at sea of her husband, Francis. It seemed to me that Martina was seen to have prospered on the back of the double tragedy, and that such a thing, locally, would have been resented. The proof of that feeling was in the way Martina totally ignored it. Whatever her own pain, she had submerged it in the business of making a success of the Ocean Voyager. I envied her the achievement. She had already shown me around the vessel, and hadn't balked at showing me the scar, still discernible in the steel of the wheelhouse, where Francis Coll died. In fact, she took a make-up kit from her purse and dabbed blusher on it, then wiped it off with a tissue so that the striae showed. Sixteen years on, and the mark still showed despite the layers of paint. But the scar on her own persona, of the double tragedy, was masked, as if brushed over with some invisible cosmetic. I had no illusion about the measure of what she had done. Many might not have seen it in the same light. But she overcame them by being herself in public at all times. She was – is – some woman!

I thought to photograph her there with her hand on the steelwork: I could have used the digital camera and enhanced the colour of the blusher afterwards, but I thought better of it and let the opportunity pass.

Keeping pace with her was a challenge.

I guess Ruan must have phoned ahead to say what we were looking for, and when we arrived she made herself instantly available. Only we left Ruan behind at the port to make contact with Owen Friel. From then on it was a magical mystery tour: hardly a turning that we didn't take, or a bog road that we failed to traverse as a short cut – near cut, they say locally. Her greeting, in some houses, was in Irish, and when the conversation flowed, I found it difficult to follow the Donegal accent. I felt out of it. It was only different to a degree when we spoke in English; she still dominated the conversation. It was as if she had never thought to do such a thing all down those years, and was somewhat guilty about it. Over-compensating! Maybe I was wrong. I have only known her since that first trip with Ruan, a couple of weeks back. But there was that one constant about her: No matter that we came up blank at house after house, her energy never failed her. If she was disappointed, she didn't show it; no more than a little intake of breath as we sat back into her BMW, and drove on to the next address in her mental list.

I could see her as a top skipper, searching every hidey-hole in the ocean, never willing to return to port without a catch.

We ate in Kilcar that second evening, Teach Bearnai's, I think it was, and we stayed late because we fell into company, but I was frustrated because we found nothing usable in our two day's searching. Only a suggestion, from the Nancy Corrigan we met, that an engineer named Niallus Coyle was big into photography, and he was at sea when we called. He was due ashore in the evening, we were told, and we arranged to call back the next day. That was the way those first two days ended, and as I went late to my room in the hotel, I paused with my fingers on the handle of Ruan's door. Would I? Would I not!

Just then, a couple passed along the corridor to their own room, and, not wanting to look like a shut out girl friend, I went to my own. But I felt shut out, and when I finally slept, I dreamt defiantly of making it with Owen Friel in some fantastic grotto in the mountains, all sun and running water. He stood me in a crystal spring and poured freezing water from the spring over me with a gleaming shell, and my nipples hardened so much that my breasts ached with the hardness of them. And the funny thing was, I was a separate being and could see myself standing in the spring, naked, as he was, and yet be a distance away. Then I couldn't see that it was me that was standing there anymore, but that it was someone else.

That's why I felt as I did on this third morning. And when Ruan finally appeared for breakfast, I told him I had something in the room to show him, and as soon as I got him inside the door, I pinned him to the back of it and tore desperately at his shirt buttons. Restraining me, he twirled the two of us about, and calmly stepped out of his clothes, then ripped everything off me, and lifting me bodily, penetrated me. And I draped my arms over his shoulders and dug my nails into his back, and bit at him. A chambermaid turned a key in the lock outside and attempted to open the door, but with an extra thrust he banged my butt against the door and closed it again.

"Not now!" he panted, and I laughed. "Yes. Now, now, now!" I answered him, and we climaxed as the door shook with the raw energy of us.

Afterwards, after we had showered and done it a second time on the bed, we went back down to breakfast again to find Martina waiting for us, and if she looked askance at our flushed faces, she said nothing. And aside from arranging to meet that evening, neither did we.

Niallus Coyle's wife was waiting for us when we got to the house – that's how it seemed – because the door opened the instant we knocked. It was a rotten morning, pissing down rain, and I was glad to get inside before my cameras got wet. There was a light on in the hall, and it made visible a picture I hadn't noticed from the doorstep on the previous day. It was an enlargement of a black and white photograph, a moonlit scene, almost certainly taken with a zoom lens; the kind of photograph enthusiasts liked to submit for competitions. It was quite accomplished, but I felt there had to be some special reason for it to be hung so prominently. I determined to ask about it. But Mrs Coyle ushered us on into her front room where Niallus himself rose to greet us.

"How's Martina?" he greeted her, then waited while she introduced me to him. He was direct.

"I believe you're after some photographs."

He looked at me.

"I'm sure you're not after just any old photographs; the 'Ocean Voyager', I imagine."

I confirmed that it was indeed the accident on the Voyager that I was particularly interested in, and briefly explained the context. At that, he gathered up and put away the albums that were lying on a casual table in front of him, and went to a locked sideboard, which he opened with a key.

"This is what you want, then," he said, taking out a thin folder. He turned to Martina. "Maybe you would prefer not to look at them." But she nodded that she would stay, and he handed me the folder.

The clarity of the sixteen year-old colour transparencies was superb. Every one of them was technically usable, but one stood out beyond all the rest. It showed one man seemingly just lying on top of another on the deck of a boat, embracing him; or wrestling with him, perhaps. The whole picture was awash with colour; green decking; sapphire sky; cobalt sea; white deck housing; ice blue ship's sides. And crimson! A great crimson gash slashed horizontally along the deck housing. Two hands and forearms dripped crimson from rails either side of the bodies, which bisected a great crimson pool on the deck. That was the picture. I said nothing, merely handed the folder to Martina. Then, I drew Niallus Coyle away, to give Martina space, and asked him about the picture in the hall.

"One of Jimmy Creagh's," he said, "you wouldn't know him. Martina might. He was cook, for years, on one of the whitefish boats. A great amateur photographer! He was the one who encouraged me when I started."

Martina had come over to us at this stage; we were standing half in and half out of the room. There were tears in her eyes.

"Can they use these, Niallus?" she asked.

"Certainly," he answered her, "and the one in the hall, if you want to; but I'll need to ask Jimmy Creagh first."

"But why would we be interested in that one?" she asked him.

His answer took our breath away.

"Because that's where Owen Friel was picked up, on the Ballinahown road."

"Jesus God!" The two of us spoke as one. "How in under God?"

He continued.

"Jimmy was returning from Dublin. His wife, you know. Well, maybe you wouldn't. His wife had some kind of an operation, and he was taking her home from hospital, and somewhere out the Ballinahown road he came on this car that had its hazard lights on. It was stopped at the side of the road, and he pulled up to ask if he could help. The driver said he had it sorted, someone who seemed to be in a bad way, but he already had him in the car, and would take him to Ballinahown. Jimmy watched him drive off. It was a moonlight night, he said, and that was when he decided to take the photograph. He always had the camera in the car."

Martina looked at me. "Holy, sweet Jesus!" she said.

Niallus Coyle finished what he was saying.

"It was only afterwards that Jimmy Creagh realised who it was that was in the car; when the news came out. The Good Samaritan must have got cold feet, because he abandoned Owen Friel in the street at Ballinahown, and was never traced. And Jimmy didn't want to get involved. I was the only one he ever told, and that was only because I complimented him on the photograph."

I'm writing all this in my journal, because nobody will ever believe me if I tell it. It's so off the wall. And the day still wasn't over.

We were making our goodbyes at the open hall-door when Niallus excused himself and returned moments later with yet another slim folder.

"The submarine!" he said, "You might need shots of the submarine."

I felt my belly warm inside me. Three massive pictures! He had just given us the front page and the entire centre spread. Talk about magic numbers. I could have kissed him, but I've been kissing too many men recently. Martina took my arm. We left. His voice followed us down the path.

"I never took Owen Friel to be up for it, in any case. He was too decent a man."

And it still wasn't over. The day mended and we called on other people, but they had nothing to offer, so we returned in the afternoon to Killybegs. Before we came to the hotel, we tracked all along the shore road, which skirted the harbour, but saw no sign of either Ruan or Owen Friel, so we eventually parked in the car-park in the 'Diamond', just outside the Pier Bar. Several of the windows were open at the top – for fresh air – and as we got out of the car, we could clearly hear the tone of some rather forceful conversation that was being carried on inside. I recognised the voice instantly, as did Martina. I moved to go on, but she motioned me to delay.

"Look, I don't know what you're talking about. What video?"

It was the answering voice that intrigued me. I had heard it before, but where? Then it hit me. It was an American voice, a woman's voice, vaguely Southern. It had the same cant as the woman on the CCTV security tape from the bar across from the Paper. Alice LaCombre! Wasn't that the name Ruan said she gave? I missed what she said, but I got his response.

"If there was a tape, I gave it to Brennan, years ago. He was a policeman, ask him for it."

I could see how it was that some policeman wanted to pin an unsolvable murder on him. He put barriers up to all questions. He kept on speaking.

"I remember you alright. You were pretty then, more than pretty; you were stunning; and even if I was drunk out of my mind I could still see it. You took advantage of me. I don't know if you ever got what you wanted. I was so drunk I never knew if I fucked you or not, or if you fucked me. You didn't take any money on me, none that I knew of. I was usually pretty secure on that front. But if it was the videotape you were after, why didn't you say so? I could have told you I gave it to Brennan."

"Come on!"

It was Martina that spoke.

"No need for us to be here, listening to useless conversations."

But her hands were clenched in fists, and the knuckles were white.

Curious, now, I hesitated. Her voice, Alice LaCombre's, came in a hard, cold hiss.

"But it's our tape, bought and paid for. We paid McMenamy for it."

Cold as her voice was, it was not half as cold as Owen Friel's reply.

"Well, ask McMenamy for it. He's not exactly in hiding."

Martina pulled me physically away, so I didn't hear what reply she made. Maybe it was just as well; I didn't want to think of the affair getting any more complicated than it was. Maybe that's why Martina pulled away also. Revenge was simpler: Kill the bastard and there's an end of it. But I don't think life, and certainly not death, is that simple. On this afternoon, Martina made a quick end of things.

"I'll pick you up at six o'clock," she said, then thought differently: "No, Better make it half past six."

And that was my day: The third day of our Killybegs search.

CHAPTER NINETEEN

OCCLUDED FRONT

I don't know why the appearance on the scene of Alice LaCombre should have bothered me so much, but it did. The trail was, suddenly, that much more complicated. Who the hell was she, really? Not some innocent American! Was she American at all? What right had she to insinuate herself into my dreams? I think it was my indignation that woke me. The morning didn't bode well. It was bucketing rain outside, and when I looked out across the harbour, I could see a tumble of white over by Benroe on the far shore. Plenty of wind outside in the bay, I thought. Where was I going to come across Owen Friel in this weather, I wondered? Full of everything negative, I made my way down to breakfast, late.

Jenny surprised me. She had already finished breakfast, and summoned me to her room, to 'show me something'. Then when she got me inside the door of her room went at me like a woman berserk. She was mad for it. It's funny, but on the previous night I ached inside with the hunger of wanting to make love to her. There, in her room, on the following morning, I saw myself as the twelve-year old Christ said of himself in the Temple: "I must be about my Father's business." But I did for her, and when the girl came to the door to do the room and turned the key in the lock, I gave extra for both of them. But it was a neck down sort of love making, and after I had showered, I made love to her again, more tenderly, on the bed to make it up to her. I'm not sure did she notice any difference.

Afterwards, we went down to the lobby and found Martina waiting for us. She made no delay, but cleared with Jenny, while I returned to the dining room in the hope of still getting some breakfast.

The dining room was on the floor above the lobby, and from my seat at a window, I had a clear view of the harbour; well, as clear a view as the rain allowed. It had eased slightly, there wasn't quite as much wind as there had been earlier, but there was still no sign of any much activity about the port. Two whitefish boats had come in out of the storm, and were discharging fish over at the auction-hall. There was a crewman on the fore-deck of each vessel, guiding the fish-boxes up through a hatch; two more on the quayside abreast of the ships, catching and stacking the multicoloured boxes as they were swung ashore. One fork truck was tending the two, lifting now from in front of one, now from the other, then wheeling in to the auction-hall. The fork truck driver was dressed from head to toe in yellow oilskins, as were the crewmen, and at the distance, and in the rain, it wasn't possible to make out who the fishermen were; only who they weren't. They weren't anyone of them, Owen Friel.

"Jesus," I thought, "where will I find him?"

Just then, my mobile phone rang. Hopefully, I flipped it open and pressed the answer button. Only at the very last minute did I look at the display. Too late! My thumb had already done the damage. I had a connection. Conaghan! His voice was cold, hard; the way it always was when he was at his angriest.

"Where are you?"

"At least he's polite," I thought.

"Still arsing about Killybegs?"

"Oh no, he's not," I realised.

"The least you could do is answer me." His sarcasm stung me.

"We're all ready to go," I told him. I lied.

"What about pictures?" he asked.

"Pictures and all," I told him, "we have some crackers." I lied again.

"We're going on Monday," he said, "either Monday or not at all. McMenamy is to appear before the tribunal on Tuesday; the Inquiry; you know, Saville. Don't let me down."

Then he asked if I had contacted Brennan yet.

"Not yet." I answered truthfully this time.

"Well do so," he said to me, "you might need him." Then he was gone. All I had was the buzz on the line.

"Excuse me, sir." It was the waitress. "Excuse me, could I clear the table, please sir."

I looked around the dining room. It was empty except for the two of us.

"Could I get another cup of coffee?" I asked her.

"In the bar, sir," she answered me. "You could get coffee in the bar, sir. It should be open now. I have to reset the tables; for the evening."

Beaten, I went to the lounge and interrupted the barman who was doing all those clearing and clinking of bottle things that barmen do in the mornings."

"Can you get me a cup of coffee, please?" I asked him, and a brandy."

When he came back with the coffee, I changed my mind. "Better make that a double!" I said.

Every so often, I walked across to a window and looked out on the bay, but there was no mend on the weather. Only cars traversed the shore road, and although I strained to see what activity there was on the Blackrock Pier, I detected no sign of Owen Friel. Frustrated by my own inactivity, I ordered another brandy. The day was going to waste on me, and I hated that. Time to brief Stephen and Mary Katherine on what's happening, I thought, and had another brandy while I mulled it over. Then, when I had my mind just about made up, I decided another cup of coffee, and a brandy might clear the brain.

"Better make it a double," I said, and I phoned Mary Katherine.

There must be a perverse Guardian Angel who defies God, and offers protection to the incurably stupid. What else could explain my safe arrival 'home'? Mary Katherine had soup ready by the time I arrived, but Stephen was the wiser and put only tea in front of me. Then, when I explained everything that was planned, and the approach I had taken with Owen Friel to gain his trust, this grandfather of mine, Stephen, opened his heart in a manner that he had never done before.

"You are flesh of her flesh," he said, " and she can only live now in you. And that is why we have loved you doubly since those two terrible days. We have loved that trace of her in you, and have loved you for yourself."

When he said that, in just that way: 'for your self', I remembered all the ways in which he did so: I had been brought up as if carried on angel's hands; allowed to make decisions for myself, secure within the protection of an intangible force field. It's funny; I had always seen Mary Katherine as the one who maintained the protective ring about me; now, of a sudden, I realised that Stephen was an even stronger power-source.

"Never forget, though that she was flesh of our flesh."

He was silent for a little while, then spoke again.

"This is your show. Whatever way you want to play it, that's OK with me. I don't want you hurt, but I think you have a better chance of getting at the truth than any of us had in this past sixteen years, and it's worth the chance. But don't shut us out, your grandmother and I; we've suffered too much heartbreak for that."

He hesitated again, and I wondered what else was on his mind.

"Jenny Stronnach's concept."

I nodded.

"Re-projecting the mind to trawl up lost visual memories."

I nodded again.

"Marvellous! But there's an easier way."

I listened to him.

"Do you think I have not searched the whole countryside, wondering where our Frances might be…."

He hesitated before uttering the word.

"…. might be buried? I know every house in the area, north and south of the road Owen Friel was picked up on. I made it my business to. Buying and selling sheep was my cover. If Owen can offer any clue at all – if he is innocent,"….

My blood chilled at the doubt in his question: "If he is innocent?" But not for a second did I doubt what he had done. A memorama of images flashed across my mind. There were days, before I was first sent to Boarding School, when I accompanied him in an old Hi-Ace van, buying ewes and lambs, maybe to sell them the following day at a mart; and moments when he stood silently, just looking around at empty landscapes. At the time, I thought it was just his way of healing himself. Paradoxically, in copying what I thought he was doing, I achieved some kind of healing myself.

" …if he is innocent, then we have some chance. But not much time if Monday is Conaghan's deadline; only tonight, or tomorrow, or the next night."

I agreed with him.

"But where the hell is Owen? How the hell can we get in touch with him?"

Mary Katherine scowled at me for saying 'How the hell?', twice, but I've heard her say worse herself and I let on that I didn't see her. Stephen said that he would track him down, and suggested that I turn in for a couple of hours.

"You might need it," he said, "we could be going tonight."

The drink I had earlier was still defying the mug of tea, so I needed little urging. I made my excuses and went up to my room.

* * *   * * *   * * *

It was good brandy; it gave no dreams, and it left no hangover; but my heart raced like a high-speed diesel when I awoke. It might have been down to my apprehension at the coming adventure, but I blamed the drink to make an excuse for myself. I was on edge. Neither Martina nor Jenny had arrived yet, and I wandered into the kitchen to ask if I could help Mary Katherine. The aroma was enticing and I enquired what was for dinner.

"Baby lamb!" she answered. "One of the late ewes had triplets. I felt she hadn't enough milk for all three, so I killed one of them. I slit its throat."

I looked at her. I didn't doubt that she had done it. I had seen her do as much before. Few had as little compunction at doing what she saw as 'practical necessities'. But I wondered this time if just such a 'practical necessity' lay behind the pre-Christian sacrifices that were supposedly demanded by Crom, the crooked one: One third of everything, and one child in every three; to prevent him taking the other two? Why I should be thinking of Crom at that particular time, I have no idea. The rain had cleared, and a sudden shaft of sunlight penetrated one of the windows, and it reminded me of a special place in the mountains above us that was dedicated to this bloodthirsty pre-Christian Sun God. Cahir Crom it was called: The Seat of Crom. This particular site was associated with mid-summer's day. Maybe I'll take Stronnach there, I thought.

"We have blood in our past, and in our present!" I said, suddenly, and for no particular reason.

"And in our future!"

Mary Katherine's response startled me, but before either of us could take it further, we were interrupted by the arrival of Martina and Jenny Stronnach, with Owen Friel in tow. I rose to let them in.

Dinner had elements of the Last Supper to it. We ate in the kitchen, and the table was strewn with odd items Martina had brought with her: An EPIRB, and a hand-held GPS device. I had seen similar instruments before, on board the Ocean Voyager, but they were shipboard instruments; not in any way as neat as the two she had with her. The EPIRB – Emergency Position Indicator Radio Beacon – was the least handy of the two. About the size of two large square torch batteries, laid end to end, it would take a large pocket to hold it securely. The Global Position System indicator was much handier. It was only just as big as one of those hand-held pocket computers, and could easily be tucked away.

But that wasn't all we had on the table.

Stephen cleared the table of plates and cutlery, and spread out in front of us an ordnance survey map of the south of the county. But before he could quiz Owen Friel as to where he thought he was picked up, Jenny trumped him with the black and white night scene of Jimmy Creagh's photograph.

"That's our starting point."

Owen Friel had paled. He picked up the picture the better to get a look at it. He opened his mouth to speak, but couldn't seem to get words to come. He looked at Stephen and handed the picture to him.

"Take it out of the frame," he said.

When that was done, both men examined it, handing it from one to the other.

"Is it?" asked Stephen.

"I think so," said Owen, "yes, I think it is. Do you recognise it?"

I looked at it myself: A half moon reflected in the surface of two lakes; the furthest away one had to be Lough Erne. I didn't think I could distinguish it from any other similar scene. But these men were different; they had skills beyond the rest of us.

"We have to try it. It's all we have."

That was Stephen, but he was overly modest. I knew what more he had.

"When?" queried Owen.

"Now, tonight, this very minute!" said Stephen, "the three of us. If we wait, we won't do it."

"What's the rush?" said Owen.

"We have until Sunday, only, to come up with something. Ruan's series runs on Monday. McMenamy testifies at the Inquiry on Tuesday. Didn't Ruan tell you?"

Stephen's answer rocked Owen back in the chair. He stared across the table at me. If he could have gotten out of it, I think he would have. But we had each dug ourselves into this. Even Mary Katherine and Martina had; and the only thing to do was dig on. Only Jenny could have cried off at that stage, and she was the bravest of all; she held with us.

"Just the three of us!" I emphasised the point.

The three women protested; Mary Katherine, because she thought we were foolhardy and ill prepared; the others because they wanted along. But we persuaded them to remain on standby on the promise of immediate contact. All three of us had mobile phones; the surprise to me was that Owen Friel had. At Martina's insistence, I took the EPIRB also. I was reluctant; it was awkward, and only just fitted into my pocket. Owen slipped the GPS into his.

"We'll go in my van," said Owen, surprising me yet again, "I have torches in it." And that's what we did. Even the weather had cleared.

CHAPTER TWENTY

MAYDAY! MAYDAY!

It was late when we left the house. The moon had risen, but was still quite low in the Southeast. It was cool. The weather forecast after the late evening news warned of clear skies and a widespread ground frost: Not all that unusual for early May. Owen drove first to his own house.

"Something I forgot," he said.

When he sat back into the van, he reached something across to me.

"Stow it away somewhere," he said.

There was a lockable document-compartment under the dash, on the passenger side. I stowed it there. It was a small-boat compass; something you might use in a twenty-footer.

He was tense, and particularly careful driving the narrow mountain road into Donegal town. He braked on every bend and on every hill. Not much practice this past fifteen years, I thought. It contrasted with tales I heard from other fishermen. Contemporaries of his, they told of wild, midnight drives from Galway to Killybegs, when the Mackerel were running down the West, when they covered the 150 miles in as little as two hours. Approaching Donegal, he surprised me by turning onto the new by-pass. It hadn't been there in his time, and I had expected him to swing in through the town. On the highway, he settled to a steady fifty-five. We might have been on cruise control. Nobody spoke. Accustomed to playing the radio as I drove, I found the silence heavy. I diddled an Irish tune in my head: Dum dum a dee di dum duma. It was half a mile further on before I could put a name to it: The Fox Chase! The phrase I was lilting was the trotting out sequence.

When we turned off the highway at the village of Laghey and took the road 'across the mountain' for Ballinahown the tension became almost unbearable. I sensed Stephen licking his dry lips beside me.

"Take it easy, now, Owen," he said.

I burst out laughing. Take it easy? What else could we do! This road was a joke. It was the main route to Dublin for the people of Southwest Donegal, yet it would have disgraced any third world country. And as for 'mountain', the highest piece of ground anywhere near was a mere nine hundred feet. But I knew what was unsettling my grandfather, Stephen, and that my own internal lilting, and the external burst of laughter, were just my way of coping with the tension; just as his nervous breaking of the silence was his way of dealing with it. I had no idea how Owen Friel dealt with his.

The last time Owen drove this road, it was in a borrowed – one might almost say hijacked – Peugeot pickup truck, and he was drunk out of his mind. In less than a week, the two labouring men, whose truck he had commandeered were dead. Their bodies were never found. Three LRA 'volunteers' were dead also – if Owen Friel's account was to be believed. Their deaths were never acknowledged. The only death given credence to was that of my mother. Her journey, also on this road, was made on the same day that the two labouring men disappeared. I was the last one in the family she said goodbye to. I can see her yet through the tears. I could still see her that night I was driving with Owen Friel and my grandfather, Stephen. In a way, it helped convince me of Owen's innocence, because I felt that if he were not innocent, I would not be able to visualise my mother. It gave me hope, too, on this wildest of goose-chases.

"Anywhere now!" The voice was Owen Friel's.

"How can he remember?" I wondered, "it must be all of sixteen years."

We rounded a small rise, but little could be seen except an edge of tallish trees, set back a bit from the fence that the road. It was then I remembered: Thousands of acres of this moor-land had been planted in Government-sponsored forestry schemes since I had started boarding school. Tracking across the moor would be next to impossible. As if he sensed what I was thinking, Stephen squeezed my elbow.

"Don't worry," he said, "We'll find the place, and the house." Then, to Owen: "Not this bend, but the next one; maybe the one after that; about half a mile further on."

But there was no rise at the next bend, and I remembered Owen's account:

"I tripped, and tumbled across the wire, then staggered down onto the road."

'DOWN'!

It had to be the 'next after' bend, but it was nearer the mile than the half. As we rounded it, it was clear the ground to our right was higher than the road, yet the falling ground to the Southeast of us allowed a glimpse of two lakes; one, some distance away, the other much closer. If it had not been for the clear night and the quarter moon, we would not have seen them at all.

"Quick! Stop! Back up a little." Stephen almost shouted, but Owen Friel was ahead of him every time.

Whatever about the years in prison, the fishing reflexes are still there, I thought. It was as if he was manoeuvring to shoot on a spot of herring. Almost before he pulled up the handbrake, he was reaching with his free hand for the pocket GPS. Stephen opened the Ordnance Survey sheet. When Owen read off the longitude figure, he lit up a flashlight and marked off a position on the map. Then he quizzed Owen.

"How many roads did you cross? Did you cross any at all? That night, I mean."

Owen hesitated, trying to remember.

"Two, I think. Yes, I'm sure of it. There were two roads; one, quite near the house, was tarred. I was afraid they'd catch me on it and I bolted clean across it. The other was just a gravel lane. I kept going on the farther side of that one as well."

"You didn't cross a railway, then?"

"When was there a railway thereabouts?" I queried my grandfather.

"Years back," he said, "but the embankments and the cuttings are there yet."

"No!" said Owen. "No railway."

Stephen was tracking his finger down the map. Satisfied, finally, he said:

"I know it. I often wondered about it. The old Boyd place. It's a two story house."

Owen Friel nodded. His throat was dried up too, I guessed. He was human. Stephen continued.

"Three or four of the windows are boarded up, have been for years, since Alistair Boyd died. He was a widower, and left no heir. There was jealousy over the land. They had killed his only son back in the thirties, and he defied them until he died in the fifties. He was a week dead before they found him in the byre. He had died tending his animals. It was the ones who killed his son were the animals. They had no luck for it. They got the place OK, by skulduggery, but they made nothing of it. I often wondered why. They were like a murrain on the place. I suppose the LRA just took it over from them."

He was silent for a moment, and it was clear to me that he was picturing the place in his mind. That was the way with him. He went on again:

It more or less faces Southeast."

Then:

"There's a bit of a lean-to at the back; a galvanised roof, I think."

Neither Owen Friel nor I said anything. Stephen caught the silence.

"Have I said something?" he asked.

"You could say that," said Owen. "You just said it."

We drove on even more slowly than before. If any local person saw us they would undoubtedly have thought us to be Travellers: Over the previous fifteen years, many isolated rural homesteads had been targeted by gangs of itinerant criminals, and any homestead in this particular area was certainly isolated. Right at this junction, left at the next fork in the road, Owen almost anticipated every instruction from Stephen. Maybe there is something in this magic number theory of Jenny Stronnach's, I thought: We were three! Finally, Stephen dipped his hand, three times in succession, signalling to Owen to stop. How he saw it in the darkness, I don't know, but he pulled up just at the entrance to a lane.

"Take it up the lane," said Stephen, "there is a bit of a bend about fifty yards up: We won't be seen."

Won't be seen! I thought. How the hell could we be seen? There wasn't a light in the landscape!

We parked. Owen doused the lights. All three of us got out of the van and stood there, eyes growing accustomed to the night sky. Gradually, the outline of a building became visible, then the roof, then even some windows. A two storey house, it was set back in an overgrown bit of a garden. From the smell of sheep droppings, it was clear the garden had not been attended in a long time. Owen took the GPS from a pocket and switched it on to check the reading. The blue-ish light of the screen glowed eerily in the darkness.

"Right on," he said quietly, "same longitude."

I reached back into the cab and took out the small-boat compass, then moved off a bit, away from the metal of the van, and rotated the luminous dial until the needle was pointing North. The house faced Southeast! I walked around the corner of the gable to check the back of the house. Owen Friel followed me. There was a single storey lean-to. I looked up and scanned the sky until I identified the 'Plough', then followed the line of the two stars that are the marker for Polaris, and faced myself North. I tried to imagine what it must have been like for Owen Friel when he crashed to the ground after he saw my mother shot dead, then raced away in a desperate attempt to escape.

Like an animal, I thought.

Suddenly, I thought to re-enact the panic of that moment, and, holding my two wrists together as if they were manacled, I crashed off into the darkness. I swear it was not pre-meditated. It was purely an animal thing, as it must have been that night. I ran as if my life depended on it. I threw myself at bushes and crashed through thickets of thorns. Briars tore at me, ripped foot-long scratches on my thighs. I clutched a torch in one hand but made no attempt to turn it on, only held my two hands together in front of me, occasionally lifting them in front of me to protect my face. Every so often, I looked up into the sky to check for Polaris, the North Star.

The two men behind me, Owen, and Stephen, my grandfather, fearful for my safety – maybe even for my sanity – called out:

"Ruan!"

"Jesus!"

Then, they too took to a run, and crashed through the night after me.

That's how it must have been with Owen, I thought, and ran all the harder, as if they were chasing me.

I must have covered all of three hundred yards when the ground rose; first, in a small ridge of rock; then plunged into a steep-sided depression. Heedless of what lay below, I jumped off the rock and found myself falling farther than I expected. I landed heavily, and my knees gave way. Struggling to hold my feet, I stumbled to one side and fell in under a bush that was growing at the foot of a rock-face.

Suddenly, I found myself falling yet again. I panicked and screamed, then hit solid ground heavily. The breath was crushed out of me, and the scream choked off abruptly. I might even have passed out.

As soon as I was conscious of anything – vaguely heard voices calling my name in the distance – I tried to call out. I couldn't even croak! It felt as if every bone in my body had been pulverised. I felt the ground underneath me; it was soft and damp; it yielded to the touch. Mercy of God, I had fallen onto a mud floor; but where the hell was I? I realised I was still clutching a torch. I prayed:

"Let it still be working!"

I tried the switch. The beam dazzled me. I waved the torch around. I was in some kind of a cave. A pothole! This was a limestone area; I had fallen into some kind of a pothole. I scanned the roof of the cave. A black cavity over my head seemed the most likely place to have fallen from. As the beam shone up-wards into the underside of a dense bush, a startled shout rang out:

"Jesus protect us!"

It was my grandfather. He must have been standing beside the bush.

"Ruan!" he called. "Ruan, are you there?"

This time I managed some kind of a shout. My breath was coming back to me. I still felt as if I had broken every bone in my back, and I groaned as I levered myself to my feet; but at least I made it. I was standing again. Then I heard Owen Friel; heard and saw him.

"You stupid, mad f***** !"

I think he didn't finish on account of my grandfather. He shone his torch down at me.

"Jesus," he said, "there's footsteps around you. There have been people down here before. Wait here until I get a rope from the van."

"No need!" I shouted back at him.

Jesus, why was I shouting? I had spotted a series of holes in the wall of the cave; a double series; steps for climbing. He juked back out from where he was lying in under the bush, and I heard him explaining to my grandfather what I had stumbled into. "I'm coming in!" I heard Stephen say, and, within a couple of moments, the two of them were at my side, dusting me off and generally inspecting me for damage. They OK'd me, and we explored the cave, following the track of the footprints.

"Orpheus and Eurydice," I heard Owen Friel murmur to himself, "in the underworld." Then, "Maybe not."

Stephen heard him as well.

"Not Orpheus, Owen!" he answered him. "Euridice, perhaps; our own Euridice – Frances. Each of us loves her, each in his own way. You, because you feel responsible for her death. Me, because she was my daughter. Ruan; Ruan, because she was the mother that was stolen from him."

He was silent for a moment, and we stood still to hear what he might say.

"The underworld! Yes, we're in the underworld. Fate has thrown us here for some reason that we don't know about, and even if we did know about it, we wouldn't understand."

What was happening was so weird, so off the wall, that we would have believed anything. That's the funny thing, we believed him. Then he said something else:

"Have you a pound coin, Ruan? My guess is that because she was murdered, nobody paid for her passage across. Nobody paid the Ferryman. That's why we're here; so that we can make good the debt."

As I said, that night we would have believed anything. I fished a pound coin from my pocket and gave it to him. He threw it in the dust.

"There's payment for you," he said to whatever phantom he had conjured up, "release her, now, from her debt."

Owen Friel took a pound from his pocket and threw it on the ground also.

"What's that for?" I asked him.

"For the other woman! The one I used as a battering ram, and as a shield. I don't know her name. She died too. I've no idea who she was, but I owe her. But for her, I would have died."

I fished one more coin out of my pocket. Angrily, I flung it backhanded into the darkness beyond the light. I didn't wait for anyone to ask an explanation of me.

"Have that," I shouted, "that's for McMenamy; prepayment!"

I think the bitterness of my anger shocked them, because no more was said, and we continued our exploration of the cave.

A shadow up ahead revealed itself, as we drew near, to be a separate chamber in which boxes and packages of stuff were stacked in untidy piles on the earthen floor. Owen Friel picked up one of the packages and turned it over to look for markings. Something was printed on the underside. He examined it, then showed it to Stephen, and he in turn handed it on to me. SEMTEX, it read, followed by some other random letters and numbers: Batch numbers or production or customer codes perhaps. We each of us looked at the others.

"Jesus Christ!" we chorused.

We had stumbled on an IRA cache. That was my first thought, then the reality of where we were and the errand we were engaged on re-asserted itself: Not the IRA, the LRA. If Owen Friel was right, this was LRA territory. The LRA: the ones who killed my mother for something – a videocassette – that they had never seen and had never even viewed. Hell mend the bastards, I thought, and said viciously to Owen Friel:

"Never mind the fucking Semtex. That's not what we are here for. We're here to find out if it was in that house that you, and my mother, were held: to find, if it is still possible, if that's where she died; and, if we have some extraordinary luck, to find her body."

Stephen reached a hand across to me and squeezed my arm, as he had done earlier in the van.

"We'll find her, Ruan, I feel it. Do you not?"

It was the way he said it more than the words that calmed me. I began to feel it myself. Fate had a hand in this: How else explain my wild flight across the moor and my tumble into the bowels of this patch of earth? He continued:

"Let Owen have the Semtex. We'll not leave it here. He may have a use for it. At the very least, he can dump it at sea. Now, let's find our way out of here. That's the greatest trick when you are in the underworld: Getting out of it!"

And that's what we did. We found the barred door that opened into a lean-to byre that was built against yet another rock-face. Stephen manoeuvred the van closer – he must have reconnoitred every square yard of ground in the fifteen years and now found a track that led to the byre – and Owen and I loaded the contents of the cave into the back of the van. When we had finished loading, Owen brushed away the tracks of the van as best he could, then went back into the cave again and barred the door from the inside. We picked him up near the house. Everything else we put on hold until we could come back in the daylight. Then we cleared. It wasn't until we were back at Mary Katherine and Stephen's house, our house, being dropped off by Owen Friel, that I missed the EPIRB. It must have fallen from my pocket when I tumbled into the cave: Either that, or during my wild chase through the scrub.

"Jesus! What if it goes off?"

No one heard my whisper, but the whole world heard the distress signal: Mayday! Mayday!

CHAPTER TWENTY ONE

BREAKING NEWS

I owe him one; Doyle I mean. He didn't have to do that. He phoned to tell me the breaking news: A plane was down in the vicinity of Lower Lough Erne. It was six in the morning. I had only been in bed about two-and-a-half hours. I was still half-asleep. He said he hadn't phoned Conaghan yet. That roused me.

"Did somebody see it go down?" I asked him.

"Nobody saw it go down," he answered, "an emergency beacon has gone off. It's on the wire. I've checked with the emergency services. They're ready to go at first light. It's not anything major like a passenger plane. They think it's something small; a private jet, perhaps."

"Perhaps," I said, "perhaps not."

I told him what we had been up to the previous evening. Not about the Semtex, mind you. I don't trust him that much. I mentioned losing the EPIRB. I had to explain that one to him.

"Jesus," he said.

"I'm coming in." I told him, "We'll be there about eleven; Stronnach and I; we can set up the opening article. This thing can work to our advantage. We could even be ready to go on Saturday. Jenny has all the pictures we need. I lied again. We hadn't got a picture of the house, and I didn't want to go back there just then.

That's what Jenny hit on when I woke her and had filled her in.

"I'm not going back there without a picture of the bloody house," she said. "Jesus, Ruan, I haven't one bloody picture of my own."

She forced me into it. I went to rouse Stephen. I found him awake and already dressed. He had heard us moving about. When I asked him if there was a height, a rise perhaps, from which the house was visible, even a half mile off, he said there was. In fact, there were two: One on the Belleek to Ballinahown road, the other on a minor country road. The second was the better of the two, he said: It had the lake in the background, and the escarpment that paralleled the South-western shore. But it was chancey, he warned:

"It's narrow. You could get blocked on it very handily."

"We'll go for it," said Jenny, "I have a big zoom in my camera bag."

She turned to face me; "I'm not going back without it."

That decided it. Within the half-hour – I was in a hurry – we were approaching a brow that Stephen had suggested was the best spot. He had travelled with us, in Mary Katherine's Espace, and had arranged for Martina to meet us in Ballinahown with my car. As we cleared the crest, two helicopters clattered low overhead, then swung away, one to either side in a search pattern. I remembered Conaghan's comment about Jenny Stronnach: "Things happen around her!" By the time the helicopters swung again, out over the lake, Jenny had already set up, and had drawn a focus on the house, then shot away as they made their grid east and west.

In ten minutes we were gone, on our way into Ballinahown. It was just at that point that Conaghan rang.

I didn't need to lie any longer.

"We're coming in," I told him, "we have all the pictures we need."

It was the first time ever I had the better of him.

It took Stephen to point out what should have been obvious to me the instant we saw the helicopters: they were British Army helicopters.

We were in the Republic, in 'the State', as the Northeners called it. The intrusion would be regarded as an incident in itself.

"I have them on camera!" said Jenny.

"The question is," continued Stephen, "what are they looking for?"

"What we found!" I answered him.

"Yes! And they won't find it, will they?"

He thought for a moment, then continued slowly.

"My guess is that they have been looking for this cache for a long time, and the EPIRB going off has given them the excuse to scout the area. They wouldn't normally be allowed fly here. Our fellow-travelling politicians are too prickly on the National Territory, every bit as much so as the 'Provos', or the LRA. What we have to worry about is what they are going to do when they find nothing."

"Maybe our helicopter will find it." This was Jenny's suggestion.

"Maybe," said Stephen, "but it had better be in daylight. It needs to be today."

I knew what he was getting at. The Search and Rescue helicopter based nearby in the Republic was grounded for night flying. An accident in the South had downed one chopper, and the western base had to rely on an older, almost-decommissioned machine. It was no longer certified for night missions. It didn't matter which of them found the hidey-hole, the LRA were bound to get wind of it. I was certain there were LRA moles in British Intelligence, and any information uncovered in the South was bound to go first to the politicians. They were collectively as sound as a cabbage colander. We needed to get the house searched. I phoned Conaghan back and briefed him. I didn't waste words. We were in the wrong place and could well have been under electronic surveillance.

"You're coming in," he said.

"We are!" I answered him.

"Both of you?"

"The two of us," I said, "Jenny needs to work on the photographic spread."

"You need someone local to cover, then?"

"Yes," I said.

"Why didn't you just say so?" he answered me, "I'll arrange it. Be on time!"

He said nothing more, but by the time we got to the city, he had the options laid out for me. He had clearly been busy. We had wasted no time, either. The change-over, of cars and baggage outside of Ballinahown, was like an Olympic baton change.

The first option was a no-no.

"We could run a bluff," he said. "We could say the authorities denied there was anything significant in the search in the Fermanagh-Donegal area. But I don't think it would work for us. In fact, I think it would backfire. The LRA would be bound to act."

I was with him on this. My fear was that they would burn the house down. They appeared to be able to move with immunity almost anywhere in the North; it would be little trouble to them to walk one man across a Donegal moor with a can of petrol.

By this time the EPIRB must certainly have been located. We had no time to lose. I could envisage the head scratching; senior officers, contacted by phone, wondering just what was involved. Conaghan dropped a bombshell:

"I'm leaving the decision up to you," he said. "It's only fair, this is personal for you," and he outlined the other options.

"Jesus," I thought, "now I have to be Solomon!"

Mentally, I felt Stephen squeeze my arm. I heard him say again:

"Don't you feel it?"

Conaghan had included a suggestion from Brennan. There was that name yet again: Brennan! Who the fuck was he really? One of these days, I had to meet him. I was avoiding him too long. He had given Conaghan a name: Inspector Starrett. If anyone was straight, he said, it was Starrett: He was head of the Border Command. He had overall responsibility for security in all the Border counties. Brennan's advice was simple: Be as truthful with him as we could, tell him as much as we felt we could safely do so.

Conaghan's hand hovered over the handset. It seemed his thinking matched mine. I hesitated only a moment. It was the most adult decision I ever had to take. What was at risk was more than just the possibility of blowing everything; I had to expose myself; I had to take someone else, a stranger, on trust.

"Dial it!" I said. I couldn't have done so myself, my fingers were crossed on both hands. I hoped nobody could see them. They were below the top of the desk.

I was sweating when I finally put the phone down. Not that it had taken long; he needed no second takes. It was clear he knew the score, even to the disappearance of my mother, and when I voiced my fear that the house could be torched before it could be examined forensically, he promised a twenty four-hour watch on it.

"In any case," he said, "we've been waiting for years for an excuse to scour this area. Not as much as a weasel will budge there for the next week without my knowing about it. Good day Mr Coll."

He ended the conversation, and I didn't think I would have cause to speak to him ever again. I'm not sure that I was satisfied, though. There was a doubt, a question, jiggling away in a dark recess in my brain: I couldn't believe that the EPIRB could switch itself on, even if it fell foul. I could see, in my mind's eye, Owen Friel pulling the disguised door at the back of the byre closed behind him. Stephen and I were on our way up the steps cut into the rock in the cave. Owen was the last to leave!

CHAPTER TWENTY TWO

THE DIVA . . .

Diary entry, May 13th, 2001.
Jenny Stronnach's journal.
This needs to be set down right away, before it dies in my mind. There is no way I could ever forget it, but that is what I want to do. I want to shut out the horror of it. I never imagined that a person could die so horribly, and in such colour: All black and crimson.

It was Ruan who asked me to write this; he reckoned he wouldn't have the opportunity to do it himself; not for a while, in any case. How does he know I can write? I wonder has he been reading my diary?

It began differently. Creating the images for Ruan's feature was a challenge, and he gave me total freedom. I demanded the front page. Conaghan gave it me.

I resurrected images I had captured at the World Surfing Championships when they were held at Donegal Bay. On that occasion, a total absence of wind created mirror-like conditions on the water, but an offshore swell gave rise to a succession of magnificent breakers, which I photographed until I achieved the effect I wanted. One blue, curling wave, ruler-straight from edge to edge of the frame. Three white tongues reached for a golden strand in the foreground of the picture. Beyond the wave, dark thickenings of colour betokened other breakers in gestation. Time spaced shots created a series of images which I combined in one print running from top to bottom of the page. It was an award winner.

For this occasion, I used the first frame and inset the faces of McMenamy and Brodie on two of the tongues of foam; the third I left untouched. Floating ethereally above this baseline, I brushed in the shipyard's picture of the Ocean Voyager taken at the sea trials. A circle at top right was filled with a head and shoulders of Owen Friel. The black banner headline read:

'GUILTY, UNTIL PROVEN INNOCENT'

I explained that I would use successive shots from my award-winning spread, as a base line for the main picture for each successive feature article. In the other frames, extra tongues of surf materialised and I thought to include additional faces from the archives as the series progressed: People, politicians, peacemakers, pop-stars: All images from the time. The visages of McMenamy and Brodie would gradually enlarge and distort as that first wave loomed larger, then morph into flecks of foam on the strand.

Doyle was dubious. Ruan shrugged. Conaghan bought it. It ran in Tuesday's paper. That was the 8th, Tuesday the eight of May. I was in Derry by then. The cover story, 'by Ruan Coll', was a direct account of the accident at sea in which his father died, and of the events on the day of the funeral. Unabridged, It was taken, virtually word for word, from Owen Friel's narrative, and it concluded with the flight to Dublin.

Reading his copy, I marvelled at how alike he and Owen were, in character and in the way they spoke. I felt it in the attraction each of them held for me. It was getting so I would have to choose between them.

The flier for the next instalment read:

"Within a week, Owen Friel would be
charged with the murder of Frances Coll.
. . . Her body was never found."

Conaghan suggested we run one of Niallus Coyle's photographs on the centre spread. It was a zoom shot of the black, unmarked hull of a submarine that had just breached the surface. O'C really has it in for somebody, I thought. I suggested insetting a second of Niallus' pictures; the shot of Owen Friel lying atop the severed body of Francis

Coll. Ruan nodded that it was OK with him, but he had to leave the office, and we heard him retching in the Men's Room. Conaghan pulled his own original report of the accident from the archives, and we re-ran that. An accompanying article, by Doyle, listed all the fishing vessels believed to have been lost in encounters with subs in British and Irish waters. The list included names of vessels that disappeared off the Belgian coast, and two in French waters.

The banner treatment given to both features was effective. They were attention grabbing. They were scary.

A further, one-paragraph news item reported 'nothing found' in the search that was being conducted in the Lough Erne vicinity of County Donegal. An unnamed police spokesman was quoted as saying that samples taken from the spot at which an activated EPIRB was found had been sent for forensic examination. The paragraph was run as a caption to one of my photographs: a shot of two helicopters flying low over a remote moor that could have been anywhere. An old two-storey farmhouse could be seen in one corner of the photograph.

For some reason, deliveries of the paper failed to make it onto the news-stands in the North that morning.

I was in Derry by then, remember.

Derry is not my favourite place. I have been there a couple of times before, and I admit it has a beautiful setting, but it is not a place I ever want to be. It is one of those places you think should be easily photographed; but if you thought that, you would be wrong. It is too divided. An artist, with his freedom to accept or reject; to include, or disregard; might fare better.

It is occupied by two tribes, and has been for centuries. It was named originally for Colmcille, that greatest of early Irish saints, full of both conflict and resolution. Doire Colmcille was the name in the original Gaelic. The 'Derry' part of it was from the oaks that grew on the island. They were sacred to the pre-Christian Irish, and Colmcille had grown up in the old tradition of the Druids and the Bards. In later life he returned from self-imposed exile on the Scottish islet of Iona to defend the old traditions. The poem written in his honour still survives fifteen hundred years later. And the Ulster planters still think they have a claim! They are one of today's tribes.

The two tribes are camped as it were, high on the steeply rising banks, defiantly facing each other, one to the East, the other to the West. The walled city, originally a hog-backed mound of an island between the two, has, over the centuries, gradually attached itself to the West Bank. It has taken sides. The swamp, in which the native Irish were obliged to live when the walled city was first built in the seventeenth century, has long been filled in, and is now known as the Bogside. The city, rebuilt after the Siege in 1690 by subscription from the city of London, and renamed Londonderry in remembrance of that, was for almost three hundred years a fortress of occupation. Not any longer! The IRA, the LRA, and the others, all 'champions of freedom', have bombed it into submission. The wonder is that the Guildhall survived. It is outside the walls.

Even those who dislike Derry rarely fail to be impressed by the Guildhall. It is a beautiful building, just outside the Shipquay gate. That's the funny thing about Derry: The finest building in it is actually outside the walls. That's where they are holding this Inquiry into what happened one Sunday in 1972, when soldiers of the British Army deliberately fired live rounds at ordinary civilians. Inquiry, for chrissake! Doesn't the whole world know what happened? They just fired on them! They killed thirteen. I would normally count thirteen as one of my magic numbers. Not in this affair! A fourteenth victim died later. I suppose I can make that an excuse; fourteen is not a prime number. It's not a good case, this; these were real people; their deaths left real pain.

Ernan McMenamy was there that day. That's why he was scheduled to appear at the Inquiry. Others were there also: The 'official' IRA, and the 'Provisional' IRA. The 'Provos' called the 'Officials' the 'Stickies'. McMenamy, of course, is now 'The Chairman' of the LRA: well he still was that Tuesday morning. Sinn Fein, the political wing of the 'Provos', has a 'President', the LRA has a 'Chairman': Mao and all that. All three organisations hated each other's guts. Hated then and still hate now. Nobody from any of the three organisations had yet agreed to give evidence to the Inquiry, except McMenamy. In this he was generally seen as trying to steal a march on the other organisations.

I travelled from Dublin on the Sunday, and met up with Ruan. He was there from earlier in the week: 'To connect with Brennan,' he said. I don't know if he did or he didn't; he never confirmed. I never asked. I didn't think it mattered. It mattered more to me that he didn't book a separate room for me, but if I expected nights – and days – like that first night and a day in Salthill, I was disappointed. Our lovemaking was perfunctory. It would have been better to sleep alone with just the ache for company. He was anticipating the day too much.

The morning of the day, May the eight, anticipated summer: The sun broke through a frosty mist that still lingered across the river in the shadows. A media presence peppered the Guildhall Square with men and women and bags, and, as the morning moved on, with discarded anoraks. Some drank coffee from plastic beakers, American style. One or two of the others were more British: They took small thermos flasks from their camera bags, unscrewed the stopper and poured their ready-milked and sugared coffee into the little cups that double as lids for the flasks. I was tempted to snap them: They were as much part of the scene as were the officials and barristers arriving for the day's session.

The photographers tended to cluster together, like athletes ready for the off. More like the long and the high jumpers, really. It was as if they had already stepped it back to a starting position that would leave them, after two or three paces of a rush, perfectly focused for their quarry. I didn't know any of them personally, although I recognised a couple from their pictures, but they acknowledged me as one of their own. Nevertheless, I hung back and a little to the side. There was plenty of light; I set my numbers for depth of field and speed. Ruan either talked with some of the reporters, who stood about in small groups, or paced nervously up and down the square. There was no sign of Owen Friel.

It was a busy, public place. Car traffic flowed constantly in and out of the Shipquay gate, which was just behind us, or turned off outside the city wall towards the Bogside. A party of tourists was addressed by a tour-guide. I presumed they were American; she spoke with an American accent. Two Japanese girls giggled as they took pictures of themselves in turn. Local pedestrians crossed over and back the square, coming and going from the direction of the Bogside, or from the bus station which was on the farther side of the road.

Suddenly there was a lull. It was almost as if it was orchestrated. No cars passed either up or down. There seemed even to be a scarcity of pedestrians, and yet, the square was quite full. A black car with darkened windows drew silently up to the kerb, just level with the entrance to the Guildhall and a heavy-set man got out. He was dark-suited, and wore heavy, dark-rimmed shades: a security man, obviously. Then, a second got out, McMenamy, and behind him came another bodyguard, also be-shaded. They moved in unison, at a measured pace, almost as if they had been rehearsed. Then, when they were clear of the car, they stopped for the press.

It's a funny thing about these 'security' people: They don't look big. Whether it is the cut of their hand-tailored suits, or the muted colours, or the black-rimmed shades that hide their features; or, indeed, the neatly trimmed hair cuts; they never look like bruisers. But you are never left in any doubt as to their ability to do you serious harm.

He was sure of himself, McMenamy was. I had never seen him in the flesh before, and I had to admit he had 'presence'. He was dressed and coifed for the occasion; the lightly greying hair trimmed to perfection and blow-dried that morning. The suit was almost certainly tailored in Saville Row: Appropriate, that. The baby-oiled and manicured hands looked as if they could never have been swabbed for traces of explosives. Even his gold rimmed spectacles had been polished. He knew how to move; how to turn and stop; how to capture attention when he halted. This was a 'Diva' performance. He had the Press eating out of his hand. He was like Christ in the Temple: hearing them and answering their questions, and they all thinking they were the re-incarnation of the wise men. All except Ruan!

I had no idea where Ruan was. As soon as the first bodyguard got out of the limo, I had started shooting away with the light weight telephoto with the wings of the lens-hood set for landscape mode, then retreated ahead of them keeping my distance. When McMenamy stopped and spoke to the reporters, I was disadvantaged. They had parted to let him through, and he turned to face them. I kicked myself for being wrong-footed. He was the Primo Tenore of this stage; no, not grand enough; the Prima Donna in person; the Diva! So experienced, he didn't need the chalk marks. On instinct, I reset the lens-hood for portrait and shortened up to general purpose.

He finished what he was saying – I hadn't taken in a word of it – and turned away from them to enter the building. A single voice, as hard as McMenamy's own, projected itself over the square. It came from somewhere behind me and a little to the right. Ruan!

"Mister McMenamy!"

It was compelling. The other photographers turned to look towards Ruan, wondering. I advanced a step or two closer to McMenamy and started shooting.

"What involvement had the LRA with the death of Frances Coll? Did you shoot her, Mr McMenamy?"

His bodyguards stiffened visibly; went on high alert. I rotated the camera, briefly, for a couple of landscape shots, then reverted to portrait mode. Somebody brushed by me on the left, and momentarily blocked my view. I fucked at him for doing so. Then, I recognised him from the back: Owen Friel! Instinctively, I pressed the motorised shoot button. The nearer bodyguard put a hand on him, to stop him. Owen turned in towards him briefly, and with a six-inch karate kick shattered his leg. It was like a gunshot going off. He must have been wearing steel toe-capped boots. Some of the reporters ducked. The noise echoed in turn from all the structures about the square, almost, but not quite simultaneously.

The second bodyguard had moved towards Owen, now turning to face him, and was stopped by the look of determination on Owen's face and a raised warning finger. I didn't see all of that, but as he turned back to face McMenamy, I saw the smile on his face, and his open, outstretched hand.

McMenamy was given no option but to grasp it.

"Smile Ernan!"

I had moved even closer, and stood astride the man who was screaming on the ground. I was close enough to hear what was said. I saw the fear that flashed, momentarily across McMenamy's face, and prayed that I had captured it. Then, his practised smile kicked in again.

"Owen, isn't it?" he asked, harshly, without seeming to require an answer, "What can I do for you?"

At a distance, it might have seemed that he had regained his composure. Close up, you would not be so sure. I snapped away, until I ran out of film. I switched to my standby camera that was hanging under my left arm.

"It's what I can do for you, that I'm here for; something you failed to deliver."

"McMenamy tried to pull away, but Owen Friel's grip seemed unbreakable. I heard McMenamy's knuckles crack.

"I'm not finished."

It was Owen who did all the talking, what there was of it.

"Alice LaCombre tells me she didn't get the video tape," – that name again! – "and I still have the original. I'll trade it. All I want is the location of Frances Coll's grave. Nothing more. Her mother has a 'geis' on me. If you don't know what that is, ask one of your Irish-speaking friends. One other thing: This is just between me and you; nobody else. You know where I live. If you don't, you can find out."

He paused.

"I'll leave a light burning, day and night."

He disengaged his hand. I saw a flash of red. There was blood on McMenamy's palm. He took a handkerchief out of a pocket to wipe it. I backed up two paces and snapped again.

McMenamy suddenly noticed me. He looked around, urgently, for his bodyguard, the one still standing.

"Get her camera!" he snarled. No more Mister Niceguy!

Ruan appeared from just behind me.

"You just can't do that, Mister McMenamy, and he pushed himself between me and the bodyguard.

"They're after my film!" I shouted at the other cameramen, and they surged forward to protect me.

McMenamy peered at the press card that was pinned on Ruan's breast.

"Who are you?" he asked, "you're the one who asked the question. What paper do you represent?"

"The 'National Correspondent'," he was answered, "and I'm Ruan Coll. If you get today's paper, or tomorrow's, you will know who I am."

Then, somebody hustled Ruan and I towards a taxi that had pulled up and was parked, with its engine running, near the corner of the Guildhall. As Ruan bundled me, ahead of him, as I thought, into the back seat, a woman jostled the man who had hustled us.

"Excuse me, Mr Gallagher." The voice – her voice – pronounced the name with a hard 'G' in the middle, like a Northerner.

Ruan started to close the door behind me, and I had just time to catch what he said:

"See you Thursday evening."

Then the hustler sat into the driver's seat and accelerated out the shore road. There was a roundabout just ahead of us and he u-turned sharply around it, then sped back along the shore road. As we drew abreast of the Guildhall again, the blue, flashing light of an ambulance could just be seen. I opened my mouth to say something; to ask who the hell he was and where the fuck was he taking me; but he put a finger to his lips and signalled caution. After about fifteen minutes driving, when we had already cleared the city, and he was sure we had not been followed, he stopped the car, got out, and searched all his pockets. Eventually, he appeared to find what he was looking for; a small gizmo that seemed to be half-plastic, half-metal. He reached again into the car and took a sandwich out of a plastic bag that was lying on the front passenger seat. He peeled the pieces of bread apart, and folded the gizmo into the sandwich, which he threw into the hedge. Then, he checked all his pockets again.

"Just in case!" he said. "With luck, a bird will get it."

He explained: The gizmo was a bug that had been planted on him. I thought back to the woman who had jostled him, and the voice. Not Northern! American! Where had I heard it before? It came to me: The CCTV security tape from the bar. The LaCombre woman! Only then did the taxi-driver introduce him self.

"Some people call me Mr Gallagher." That was the name on the taxi. "It suits me to let them," he continued.

Walking around the car, he rapped on the lid of the boot.

"Not yet," he said, "another couple of miles."

Then he got into the car and drove on across the Border, in the direction of Letterkenny.

About three miles on the other side of the Border, he turned abruptly into an entrance and pulled to a halt in a yard at the back of a two-storey farmhouse. We were well hidden from the road: The house itself could scarcely be seen, set back as it was behind a tall, unkempt hawthorn hedge. A woman came out of the house. The man "some people" called Mr Gallagher, got out of the car and went round to the boot, which he opened with a key. A very cramped-looking Owen Friel climbed stiffly out of the boot.

"Jesus!" I exclaimed, "How was that done?"

I got out of the car myself. 'Gallagher' motioned us urgently towards a dirty white van that was also parked in the yard. The woman sat into the back seat of the taxi.

"Quick," I almost shouted at her, "Where is there a toilet?"

The whole thing was too much for me. I'll have to give up this job; at least give up on encounters with Owen Friel. The adrenaline was pumping in me. I was close to pee-ing myself again. The woman waved towards the door of an outside loo.

When I had relieved myself, and re-emerged pulling up the zipper of my jeans, Owen Friel was shaking hands with the taxi-driver. It was a funny, two-handed shake; not quite like the politicians' false greeting of hand and elbow; and not like the brothers' hand and wrist, look-no-weapon type of handshake; it was much more careful. Then he walked to a tap at one side of the back door and ran it to wash his hands and I understood: I could see traces of blood on them, and remembered McMenamy. Owen showed me his hands. Sharp chippings of a vaguely flesh-coloured stone appeared to be stuck all over his palms.

"Superglue!" he said, and he grinned. "The only way to catch an eel! With a handful of grit."

He hustled me into the van – this was getting to be too much hustling - and explained that Brennan would drop the woman, in my place as it were, at the bus station in Letterkenny.

"Brennan?" I challenged him, "Surely you mean Gallagher!"

But he didn't. He didn't explain much either; only that Brennan was pressured into leaving the Force. It was something about a book of evidence, and the videotape, going astray. It sounded as if there was an O'Hara involvement, but what he wouldn't say. He switched back to the present and that was an end of the explanation.

He did explain the woman; she would be a decoy, as far as Letterkenny. She could then catch a bus back to Derry and be dropped off at her gate.

We followed out the road after them, but turned off at the next fork. Owen Friel said it would take us down through Raphoe and Convoy to Ballybofey and the main road for Donegal Town.

I thought of the lake on the high moor above Ballybofey; the belly and the navel of County Donegal; and the fast plunge into the great gap east of The Blue Stacks. It was a sexual landscape; the sides of the gap like two great thighs. I was still hot with the adrenaline rush from the ambush – what else was it? – in the Guildhall Square, and I wasn't at all sure I wanted to be in that van with Owen Friel on that particular day. I was in too high a state of sexual excitement.

CHAPTER TWENTY THREE

... AND THE DANCE

I shook her when she told me. I pulled her after me to a car park, in at the back of the shops, that almost no one uses so isolated is it, and I shook her a second time. I banged her against the galvanised tin of an old shed.

I wish I could shake her again. I asked her to write this bit of the story. I was too close; too involved. But she gave up on it. She started, and got so far, then gave up. Maybe I shouldn't blame her, she's no stronger than I am. Damn Owen Friel. If it weren't for him!

None of this would have happened: That's what I was going to say, but I don't know if that's true. I only know I can't go back and change the past. If I could do that, I would have no submarines. That's how it all started. Maybe that's not true. Was my father's ambition just a factor? And Mary Katherine's ambition! It too? Truth is, there is no one point to which we can go back, and no one point to which we can advance in the future, either. There is only the here and now. That is what all of us deal in: The here and now. That is what I was about when I shook her.

She had taken a lift to town, to meet me coming in from Derry, from Stephen. He had an errand of his own to tend to, and dropped her off in The Diamond. When I saw her, there was something about the look of her. Something that said she had things to hide. That's what made me challenge her.

She lied to me.

"Did you fuck him?" I asked her, and she said she did.

I banged my fist so hard on the corrugated, my knuckles bled.

How well she described the place! A humpback bridge just off the main highway above Bearnas Gap: A bit of a holly-bush struggling for survival at the side of the bridge: A minor road, scarcely more than a tarred track crossing the bed of an abandoned railway, disappears from sight behind the rise of an embankment. The landscape is full of visual tension. It is reminiscent of a scene from that old movie they keep playing on television: Shane. I can see it still. And the tension between him and her!

"Did you fuck him before?" I asked her, and she lied to me again. She said she did.

"Jesus, where?" I quizzed her.

"In the hotel in Athlone," she answered. "You put me in bed with a naked man; remember?"

She paused.

"And he wasn't dead, you know."

That did it. That was too much. I banged her against the shed again and again, until I became afraid I would kill her. Then, I locked my two arms around her and held her, for fear I would, just, do that.

I cried dry, bitter tears of frustration. I didn't know what to believe anymore.

I wanted to take her back out the road again, to that lonely place above the Gap, but instead, I threw up all over the bonnet of some car that was parked there.

Eventually, when I got control of myself again, I drove her up the road home to Mary Katherine's, where she had been stopping since Owen Friel dropped her off. Neither of us spoke. But later, when everyone was asleep, that night and the night after, she came to my room and we made love once, quickly. And then we indulged in an orgy of lovemaking, and I didn't care what stains Mary Katherine might find on the sheets. It was on that second morning that Mary Katherine said I had better tell Jenny to throw her bags into my room: She was fed up with people creeping through the house at night while she was trying to sleep.

If the nights were hot between us, the days were cool, and we didn't face into what we should have been doing. Maybe Mary Katherine noticed, but if she did, she made no remark on it. She waited for us on the second morning, so that we could accompany her to Mass, and sniffed "Though what good it will do you pair of debauchees," as we entered the chapel. It stung. She challenged us, Mary Katherine did, and after Mass, we spread Jenny's photographs on the big living room table and established a conference link to Conaghan. Mary Katherine took herself off to the kitchen. Stephen was out the hill since early morning and hadn't returned yet. Owen Friel arrived with Martina, but went into the studio in the annexe about their own business, and we paid no heed to them.

Jenny had couriered the negatives to Conaghan, having taken her own prints first, and we rowed about that, because I wanted to do the whole thing from the house. But we hadn't got a broadband connection, and I couldn't argue for a poorer quality picture.

"Trust me," she said, but I was in a humour to trust nobody.

Her pictures were tremendous. No one had ever captured McMenamy with fear on his face before. It made him vulnerable. But one photograph stood out from all the others: The snap of him washing the blood from his hands. As an image, it said everything. It suggested it's own caption, 'Pilate, innocent?' Conaghan disagreed. Drop the 'Pilate' he said. That's what he went with:

INNOCENT?

The picture would run the full depth of the front page, set left, and under the banner, he proposed the crunch question:

'What involvement had the LRA in the death of Frances Coll?'

It was scurrilous journalism. I had no problem with it.

Inside – he insisted on giving us the entire centre spread again – he went with our suggestion to re-run the picture of the house and the helicopter search on the moor, with a banner:

'IS THIS THE HOUSE WHERE FRANCES COLL DIED?'

I was satisfied. I didn't even have to write the copy. Doyle wrote it.

Stephen came in from the hill before we were finished, and when he saw what we were at, washed his hands and went to his room. He returned with an old school photograph, and named for us some of those who were in it: Francis; Frances; Owen Friel; Anthony Killoge; Martina. We scanned it in, ringed the five, and e-mailed it to Conaghan: To be used as an inset, we told him.

After we had e-mailed it, Stephen pointed out one other:

"Martin Brennan," he said.

Jenny lifted the photograph and walked across to the window to the light, the better to see it.

"Well, well," she said, "Mr Gallagher himself!"

She pronounced it with a hard 'G' in the middle, like a Northerner.

Nothing happened that day, on the Saturday.

Sunday morning brought an occluded front that stretched from Donegal to Kerry. Nothing unusual in that: Mary Katherine's island kin depended on the 'May seaweed' as fertiliser for planting the late potatoes. But this was different. Savage downpours punctuated the day. Odd cracks of thunder rumbled in the distance. In the showers, the rain lashed the front windows as if it were March. We lunched at one end of the table without disturbing the snaps, which were still spread out from the evening before. The air almost crackled with the static in the air, and after lunch Mary Katherine excused herself and went for a lie down. Jenny cleared the table and did the needful with the dinner things, then joined me in the window seat. Stephen sat at the end of the table, idly looking at the photographs.

The afternoon went in like that. When the sky darkened and the rain struck the window, we shrank in a bit. Then, when it cleared and brightened again, Jenny would rise and stroll to the table, and move back to the light, peering at some photo or other. Nobody spoke. It started to bug me. When she crossed the floor for the eleventh time, it got too much.

"Jesus!" I exploded. "What's this, a mixed-excuse-me or a fucking lady's choice?"

"Ruan! Wash your mouth!"

This was Stephen. It was years since he had to speak to me like that. I was lucky Mary Katherine wasn't there. She would have scalded me.

I apologised.

"What do you know of 'lady's choice's or 'mixed-excuse-me's in any case?" he asked me, "they were before your time."

"You reared me!" I answered, ungraciously, and was immediately sorry for doing so.

Embarrassed, Jenny rose and gathered up the photographs and took them with her to the room. She didn't come back.

Towards evening, the weather seemed to ease. Mary Katherine came from her room and tended the small turf fire in the cluid that she had set earlier. She made some tea, a cup in the hand only. Afterwards, we sat watching the television: Me in the window seat, Stephen at the table, Mary Katherine in her favourite seat in the cluid. From time to time, the screen sparked and blacked out, then fizzed back to life again.

"The thunder's still about," she remarked.

The sky darkened over in the Southeast, and the glow of distant lightning flashes brightened the sky beyond the shoulder of the hill. It was a distance away, but the peals of thunder could still be heard, rumbling like stones in the surf. The storm intensified.

"It's over by Ballyshannon, I think."

Stephen was probably right, I thought. That was where the Erne hydroelectric dam was at, and the regional power station. That's why the TV crackled.

Suddenly there was an almighty spark and the power failed completely. Immediately the emergency lighting cut in. Mary Katherine had been obliged to install the system, for insurance purposes, because she used the house, and the studio in the annexe from time to time, for public entertainment. She had included a couple of lights, at the door and on the path outside, also. These now lit the approach to the house.

After a few moments, I heard the sound of footsteps and Jenny appeared on the landing; only a shape, really, in the half-light, and made her way carefully down the stairs. She was carrying what appeared to be a boxy torch, and she crossed over and sat beside me in a corner of the window seat. Nobody said anything, only watched the reflections of the lightning in the sky outside. Nothing else could be seen, only darkness, on the hillside above us where Owen Friel and Anthony Killoge's father lived: Nothing only blackness.

After a while, the lights of a car appeared, making its way up the road below us. The beams of the headlights sliced the night before it as it twisted and turned with he contour of the hill. Reaching the gate below, it turned into our 'street' and drove around the corner of the building.

"Jesus!" I said to myself. "It's McMenamy!"

I remembered Owen Friel saying in Derry that he would leave the light burning, "day and night." Ours was the only house lit.

Stephen rose from his chair at the end of the table. I heard the latch of the door click as it was released, and a wedge of brightness from the outside light expanded into the room. Then it was all but blocked off by the dark silhouette of a man's figure; and, as the man stepped into the room and carefully closed the door behind him, the wedge shrank to nothing and was gone.

"Come in, Mr McMenamy." This was Stephen. "I'll just go and get a better light. I'll only be a moment."

Stephen picked his way down into the kitchen and we could hear the sound of him footherin', moving things around on a shelf, or in a cupboard. I caught the smell of methylated, and shortly afterwards there was the splutter of a match and a small flicker of flame. It seemed that he hardly waited long enough for the paraffin to heat, but when he pumped up the pressure, the gas ignited right away, and the hissing, white light of the 'Tilley' lamp' bloomed inside in the kitchen. Then there was the sound of a more vigorous pumping, and the scrape of furniture on the stone floor. Blinded by the light, he must have backed into a chair.

McMenamy was silent all this time. We all were. I wondered at him not excusing himself and moving to go. I wondered that he didn't see and recognise the photographs that were hung either side of the chimney-breast. Surely he must have seen the short-hafted pike resting on the granite pegs set into the stonework above the cluid, and been intrigued by it. It caught my own eye and I was intrigued: I couldn't recall Stephen taking it from it's hiding place down in the room. Maybe McMenamy thought this a nationalist house; 'Republican' even. But his eyes scanned the room, nevertheless, peering, trying to figure out, who all were there.

Stephen made his way back from the kitchen. I heard the sound of his footsteps on the flags, and shadows flickered into the room. He was carrying the Tilley lamp in his left hand, and he paused just inside the door, a little short of the other door leading to the annexe. Slowly he lifted the lamp and placed it carefully on a mantel just to the left of the cluid. He set it immediately in front of the photograph of my mother. She was pictured wearing a white shirt and jeans. Her blonde hair was flattered by sunshine of the day it was taken, and she was laughing. I never knew, not till later, that they were the clothes she was wearing the day she was murdered.

The second picture; a photograph of Martina, which was hung further to the right; was shaded by its frame. Mary Katherine must have been almost invisible in the shadow in the cluid, Jenny scarcely less so in the corner of the window. Stephen moved on into the room, back to his usual place at the end of the table, and sat into a chair.

As McMenamy's eyes became accustomed to the light, he scanned the room yet again. Eventually, his stare settled on the photograph. I heard the soft intake of breath, and then what he said, even if it was only a whisper:

"Jesus! I've come to the wrong fucking house!"

"Wrong thing!" I thought. Mary Katherine heard him as well.

"Wash your mouth, Mr McMenamy!" she said from her seat in the cluid, and she rose to face him. "I'll have none of that locker-room language in this house."

This was Mary Katherine: Earth Mother: Defender of the hearth: Protector of the place that was the beginning and the end of life, the cluid. It was there, the cradle was warmed; there also, the old ones lolled in their rocking chairs.

She challenged him:

"Was it you that killed my daughter, Frances, Mr McMenamy?"

His answer was cold as ice water.

"No Ma'am," he said. "It was Brodie!"

She didn't let him away with it.

"Was it you, Mr McMenamy that called it? Was it you that shouted for her to be killed?"

He was brazen.

"She wouldn't give us what was rightfully ours."

He had slipped his right hand into the pocket of his jacket, and now withdrew it, holding some kind of a pistol. I can remember marvelling at the skill of his tailor, that he could cut and fashion a suit pocket to conceal such a thing.

Mary Katherine just turned and lifted the pike down off the pegs above the cluid, then turned back to face him.

"Jesus!" I said to myself. "This is madness." Torn between wanting to protect both my grandmother and Jenny, I moved to place myself between McMenamy and Mary Katherine.

"Does he think he can kill us all," I wondered, "and get away with it?"

I put my hands on the pike to try to take it from her. She pulled away from me and stepped to one side, still to face him.

"And what was so rightfully yours, that she had, that she wouldn't give you?"

There was fire in her voice.

"Whatever we wanted," he answered. "She had no right to keep anything from us."

"And for this, you killed her? For no good reason, by your whim only, you destroyed our daughter; you took everything from her, even life itself. You took her from us who loved her. You took her from my grandson here, who had nothing left in this world only her: Because she wouldn't give you what she hadn't got to give…   Some imagined thing on a videotape…"

She paused.

"Do you think you can kill us all, Mr McMenamy?"

He sneered at us.

"As easy the dam as the bitch," he said, "or the whelp."

Her eyes flamed with anger. I could see Hell itself in them. She snatched the pike back out of my grasp and raised it high.

Suddenly, the door exploded inwards, and the figure of Owen Friel burst in. This was Greek Tragedy married to Grande Guignol.

Owen Friel was out of breath, as if he had been running. His hair was wild and stood in dark spikes, like bare blackthorns in winter. He was brandishing what looked to be a garden fork, but I recognised it for what it was, a turf grape. He must have picked it up as he was passing the turf stack. There were steel balls welded onto the end of the tines.

I never saw a man to move so fast. All the TV images had deceived us. We were too accustomed to seeing him move slowly, or not at all. A practised deception!

"McMenamy crouched low and spun around backwards, turning with the sun. His right arm slid under the turf-grape, knocking it up and harmlessly out of the way. Then he smashed the barrel of the gun on the side of Owen Friel's head. He dropped like an animal that had been pole-axed.

The boom of a gun going off froze everyone into stillness. A bullet shattered some ornament of Mary Katherine's on a shelf beside the door. In the confined space, it was like a shot from a cannon. Stephen had fired what looked to be an American style automatic. It looked enormous, probably a forty-five; I wouldn't know. A relic of his time in Korea, perhaps.

Time stopped.

In the stillness, the sound of another door opening, in another part of the house, could be heard. The old, iron hinges were dry, and creaked for want of oil. The door of the annexe! Somebody was in the studio! Footsteps echoed from the conservatory passage. Light footsteps. A woman; it had to be! There was an audible click as the latch was lifted. The plank door from the conservatory passage into the room opened ever so slowly, and folded backwards into the darkness. A blonde-haired figure appeared. It was a woman! She was wearing jeans and a white top of some kind. It was more shirt than blouse. The two top buttons of the shirt were open at the neck. There was a hole in the shirt just over the left breast, and a crimson stain was spreading across the white of the fabric.

As I live, it was my MOTHER!

JESUS! IT WAS MY MOTHER!

As I live and die, it WAS my MOTHER, walking into the room.

"Oh, Sweet Jesus, mercy."

That perfect white breast that suckled me was a red oozing mess.

Then the whole thing turned into a bizarre 'Danse Macabre'.

Jenny Stronnach rose from her seat in the corner of the window. The thing that I thought to be a boxy torch, I could now see was one of the very latest digital video cameras. She moved out into the light to get a better view of what was happening.

McMenamy had turned to face the figure that had just entered the room and was staring in disbelief. When Jenny stood up, his head swivelled back to her. His eyes flickered with comprehension.

"The fucking bitch photographer!"

My mind had locked onto his. I could hear what he heard; see what he saw; think his thoughts. Image was everything. The media and the photographers, when you controlled, when you could manipulate them, built that image for you. When they took the wrong pictures, when they could not be controlled, they became the destroyers, and needed, themselves, to be destroyed.

I saw his finger whiten on the trigger.

I wrested the pike from Mary Katherine again. Jumping backwards, like a shot-putter gaining impetus, I whirled like a dervish.

"Duck!" I shouted at Stephen, and swung the pike in a great rising arc. The blade caught one of the four hanging lamps and sheared the flex in the instant. The lamp crashed to the floor. Then I pulled hard down on the shaft and released my grip.

It was a trick Stephen was shown by his grandfather, and passed on to me.

The pike flew outwards, until my hands fastened again on the stopper knot that Stephen had bound around the butt of the shaft. The blade bit into McMenamy's neck, just above the collarbone, and the tine lodged in one of the vertebrae of his neck. It stuck fast. I shortened in my grip and shook the pike until the vertebra broke, then drew the blade onwards out of the wound. I didn't care whether I cut him more or less.

I think everyone stood still for an awfully long time.

When Owen Friel recovered sufficiently to get up, he stumbled on the shattered lamp, then steadied himself somewhat and looked at the body on the floor.

" I didn't want him dead," he said.

My response was even shorter than his:

"I did!"

Nobody else spoke.

CHAPTER TWENTY FOUR

POST-FATAL DEPRESSION

Everything changed in that moment. I thought the burden of losing my father in a terrible accident at sea; and of my mother being murdered, never to be found; was a bad deal. Nothing compared with killing a man. I was grateful for the half-darkness of the lamplight: The others could not see my face as they might have done in daylight. We all stood for some moments in silence.

After a few minutes, the power came back on again. They must have re-established the circuit in Ballyshannon. Immediately, the bared ends of the severed flex from the hanging lamp shorted. Blue sparks created a crackling blue light that lasted no more than seconds, then the power failed again. The ELCB tripped out. Stephen made his way out into the kitchen, where the fuse-board was, and threw the switch. This time, the connection held; the wires must literally have burnt themselves apart, and suddenly we could see properly again.

But the light made no difference to those feelings that had come instantly to me in that moment of darkness. Nothing could ever be the same again. I could see it in the faces around me. No one looked at me. If ever I was alone it was then. It gave me no choice. I determined I would halt this murrain before it could develop further; I would stop it ever becoming a cancer.

I looked at each one in turn, unblinking, until each in turn acknowledged me by looking back. I put my two arms around Mary Katherine and embraced her.

"My mother can rest, now!" I said.
I reached my arm out and rested a hand on Martina's shoulder, no more than that. I had realised by then that it must have been Martina – wearing a wig – that became temporarily my mother.

When I looked at Owen Friel, he was frozen, and as pale as moonlight. He was staring at Martina. He was transfixed. Even when I put my hand on him, it was as if he scarcely even knew I was there. But his hand caught mine.

"Jesus, Ruan," he said. "That's the way she was. I never thought to see her ever again."

His voice was a whisper. When he spoke again, it was even lower.

"I let her down, and you, leaving her like that."

There was no answer that would have satisfied him, so I pressed his hand in the two of mine and went out to the kitchen, to Stephen. He was leaning with his two hands on the kitchen table, trembling uncontrollably. I felt he was glad it was me that came.

"I thought I had lost Mary Kate, Ruan. The God's truth, I did. The gun jammed! I don't know what I would have done if he had killed her."

The now useless gun was lying where he must have thrown it when he came into the kitchen: on the table.

Only then did I go to Jenny. Stephen followed after me. Jenny was still holding the camcorder and still standing in the same spot she was in when I struck out at McMenamy. She was shivering. I folded her into my arms and held her tight for a very long time. Eventually, as I drew away from her, I realised that a great red weal ran diagonally up along the side of her neck.

"Jesus! You've been shot!"

For once, I got away with it.

"Where? The creature! Here, let me see." Mary Katherine took over, and let my expletive go. Stephen showed me the two bullet holes, only six inches apart, that had drilled the window. A third bullet must have been loosed at Mary Katherine; either at her or myself: It had shattered the glass in the framed photograph of Martina.

It was only then, I realised, that McMenamy had actually fired.

'What… 'What a….. 'What a man!' I wanted to say, because Jenny was more of a man than any one of us, but the words wouldn't come. It was not just that she was so completely professional. She was too much a woman for me for me to think of her in any other way and I was besotted with her. Just at that moment, I wished there were nobody else there but us. I looked round jealously at Owen Friel, but Martina had gone to him and was tending to his needs. He peeled himself away and said:

"It's time to call Starrett, I suppose."

For the second time that night, I disagreed with him.

"You suppose wrong, Owen. Nobody calls Starrett until I have an extra copy of what's in that video camera, be it on tape or disc. Then we can call Starrett!"

That's the way it happened: Well, not quite. Mary Katherine took a hand in it. She insisted on calling her solicitor, a Mr O'Donnell, first, and had him call Starrett, to dictate her terms: She would surrender and vacate the house, but only to Starrett himself. Nothing would be touched. Mr O'Donnell would arrange for a junior to be present as an observer while a forensic search and examination took place. She would arrange a suite of rooms for us in one of the hotels in town, and we would, each and every one of us, be available there for interview.

"One last thing, Mr O'Donnell," she said, "I want a forty eight hour stay on the release of the news to the media."

O'Donnell must have quibbled.

"Well," she answered him, "twenty four hours, then. I'll accept twenty four."

He must have hummed a bit, because the tone of her next response was sharp:

"Tell him I'm instructing you to initiate a case for the wrongful arrest, conviction and imprisonment of Owen Friel in the matter of the murder of my daughter, Frances Coll. Tell him. Tell him that, Mr O'Donnell."

It was outrageous, but she got away with it. She even got the twenty four hour stay, but she had to threaten to campaign for an Inquiry as to why a certain, named police officer was obliged to leave the force. Without a doubt, she left Starrett's neck on the block. This was political Semtex.

Jenny smuggled the DVD out of the house, stuck down the front of her knickers, while I ran a diversion. Later, she managed to sneak out of the hotel, and phoned Conaghan from a card-phone in the 'Diamond'. That's what they call open public spaces in Donegal. Conaghan arranged a drop point for her, for the following evening, but in the event, he had Brennan pick her pocket in the street. She was mad about that, but it was his way of being ultra careful. He had the disc by Tuesday, midday.

Stephen saved his negotiation for the police interview. He was the first to be processed, by Starrett himself. Always the epitome of cool reason, his account set a tone that allowed the rest of us later escape the severity of interrogation that we perhaps deserved. Of course he had to explain the gun: It genuinely was a relic of his time in the American Forces in Korea. But it was the supporting video that confirmed he used it only in an attempted defence of his family; and it had jammed!

What he bargained for, was an enhanced effort to discover the body of my mother, which he was convinced was buried near the farmhouse on the moor. That, and the participation of two brothers of Mary Katherine in the search. Poteen makers all their lives: No one, he believed, knew more about hiding things in the earth, or of finding them again. Starrett agreed. I thought him a decent man.

I'm certain it was hardest for Owen Friel; after all, he was there before. Starrett gave him no easy ride; fifteen hours of an interrogation, from eight in the morning until eleven on that first night; eight hours on the second day. But he didn't enquire too much into why Martina was already rigged out as my mother. That was something I wondered about, myself, but let pass. He was my Godfather. Not that I had the opportunity to quiz him on it. I was facing my own interrogation. Fifteen hours the first day – I think they switched teams between us every so often – and eleven the next. But I told it as it was, again and again, and again. In the end, they had no option but to accept it. Jenny Stronnach's video recording was irrefutable. Owen Friel was bound over, as I was. We were both required to surrender our passports – I was surprised to learn that he still had one – and to report daily to a named police station. We both nominated Killybegs.

Conaghan ran the 'Derry' picture, and the second part of the feature, exactly as planned on the Tuesday. Starrett had been as good as his word. The news of McMenamy's death hit the wire only just in time for the 4 a.m. late city edition, and even then, Conaghan only ran it on an inside page.

All hell broke loose. Starrett must have felt as if he were the only defender of Stalingrad in World War Two. I wouldn't have known about that, only that there was a Hollywood film of it doing the rounds. Extraordinarily, my mobile phone, which I had surrendered for checking, was returned to me the same afternoon, and in the evening I locked myself into a toilet in a corridor in the hotel, and phoned in my 'eyewitness' copy. I wondered if it was usable. Conaghan's answer was, more or less, 'to hell with obstruction of justice', and printed it. It made its own headline on the Wednesday, but only on the centre spread. The cover carried an enlarged still taken from the DVD. It showed the blade of the pike just after it severed the flex of the hanging lamp. A tongue of flame spouted from a gun that had been fired from somewhere at the back of the picture. The face illuminated by the finger of light was McMenamy's. The banner simply said:

JUSTICE

Conaghan told me afterwards, he was tempted to go with the headline 'Lights out', but he thought it too flippant.

It was a sensation. Picked up internationally, and syndicated on all five continents. The Middle Eastern countries, especially, took it; but their primary colours seemed to be red and black and grey. Much later, Conaghan showed me one of the most lurid. It reminded me of pulp fiction covers on old 'forties and 'fifties paperbacks in Mary Katherine's library. For no reason, the name of one of them, an Irish language adventure, kept repeating itself in my mind: 'Reics Carlo agus An Tir Fo Thuinn' – Rex Carlo and the Land at the Bottom of the Sea.

It was Thursday before they released the house to us. I can still see the look on Mary Katherine's face as she reviewed the damaged plank door on its skewed hinges, and was close enough to hear her muttered "Fluther!" It was the closest I ever heard my grandmother come to swearing. O'Casey's play, 'The Plough and the Stars', opens with a character named Fluther Good fixing the door.

No fault to Conaghan, but I was unusable, an embarrassment. True, he phoned me every day, but it would have suited to have a foreign war to send me to. With luck, I could have covered myself with glory, or get blown up, or, better still, both! Instead, I found myself in Killybegs, working alongside Owen Friel.

I was pleased enough to be working with Owen. Pleased enough, also to get the daily calls from Conaghan. What we were doing, rigging trawl gear, wasn't exactly mindless; the eventual success of the trawl depended on it, but the repetitious chuck, chuck of knots and lashings being tightened saved me from thinking. Then, as each stretch was completed, I could indulge myself in a few moments of dream-time. I saw oceans beyond ours, and my mother and father walking the bridge of some grand vessel, hand in hand, only for the image to fade, and find myself alone in a coracle.

I was up and down, like a bird in a gale. Owen understood, and whenever I stopped, seemingly unable to go on, he was patient, and waited until the mood passed. It's the "hungry grass", he said on one occasion, "but not in the physical sense. It's in the metaphysical." I thought that was why he arranged to have an extra man, Anthony Killoge's father, with us the following week.

He was a nice man: A neighbour to us all my life, and about the same age as my grandfather. As active as him, too. He fished himself in the old days, and he regaled us with stories of characters long gone. He travelled in with Owen in the white van. I envied Owen for that, because he was such good company. Even so, I preferred to drive myself.

There was another excitement to the week. Owen took delivery of a new long-line winch, for tuna. It arrived ready spooled with what Owen said was sixty miles of nylon line. It looked it. Over two metres wide, and a metre something in diameter, it looked special; the line itself more a white wire than a twine. When the fork trucker lifted it off the lorry, Owen had him take it to a store he had rented; a big shed, really. It blocked up the entire front of the shed.

I was suspicious about what else was in the shed. There was a stack of bags on a couple of pallets in at the back, but I couldn't get near enough to see exactly what was in them. Salt, I presumed, but the bags were half-covered by a tarpaulin, and though I suspected they hid the Semtex that Owen had taken from the cave on the moor, the stream of fishermen who came to wonder at the tuna-winch allowed me no opportunity for any surreptitious investigation.

It didn't help that Conaghan phoned about that time, and quite plainly asked me to keep an eye on Owen.

"Fuck off," I shouted down the phone at him.

It was bad enough that I had become a killer; now I was to be a 'stoolie!'

He got my attention, though, when he mentioned the text message advertisements that had appeared in the paper. I hadn't been reading it, deliberately, and had missed them. The first ran:

"BrD, wnt rng. nt ntndd. stl 1 2 Dl. OF"

The answer, a couple of days later, he said, was:

"It all B"

The tuna long-lining puzzled me at first. Tuna had only been fished in Ireland, in the Southwest, for about eight or ten years, and there, only with gillnets. This kind of long-lining was used elsewhere, but as a floating line. Owen had us pull off sixteen measured lengths of the heavy nylon filament – something over 100 fathoms in each – then got us to make up sixteen heavy concrete weights. Floating lines, yes; bottom-set lines, definitely not.

The following morning he appeared with a box of small electrical gadgets; transponders, he called them, which he said were for the lines. He had them specially assembled in a local electronics company. When the fish rubbed against the lines, the transponders would transmit a signal, he said. Anthony Killoge's father reminisced about old-time herring fishermen that used piano wire, before they had echo sounders, to 'feel' for fish. It was like the light coming on in Mary Katherine's all over again: that same spooky feeling. This thing was not over yet. And the sensor lines were not for fish: Not in any conventional sense, in any case. Tin fish, maybe. Submarines!

But where did Brodie fit into all of this? I couldn't figure it, and I got no chance to.

I came late on Saturday morning and found no one at the shed before me. I scanned the harbour and the shore road. The bigger pelagic vessels were tied up, season over, at the main pier. They included the family's 'Ocean Voyager', which had offloaded all the fishing gear in preparation for a trip to a yard in Spain. The medium and smaller pelagic boats were tied two-abreast at the Blackrock pier. Two whitefish boats were discharging at the auction hall, and there was the usual clatter of winches and hurry with fork-trucks. But of Owen Friel, and Anthony Killogue's father, not a sign.

I drove to the small boat berth: Not a trace of Owen's vessel!

"Jesus," I cursed myself.

I raced to the shed and forced my way in. The nylon buoy lines, and the weights, were gone; buoys also. The box of transponders was missing. At the back of the shed, the bags of salt had been scattered, hurriedly, by the look of it, and whatever was under them had gone as well.

No time for cursing, I phoned Martina on the mobile: told her what had happened and what I suspected. She did the cursing for me.

"I'll be there in twenty minutes," she said, but made it in fifteen. John, the skipper of the 'Voyager, made it in ten. The engineer took a little longer. In another five, we had cast off and gone.

"Where to?"

That was all John asked as we cleared the harbour. It was clear he had been a long time with Martina.

"You know where my father died? Is it still in the memory?"

I meant the navigational computer.

"Seared into it!"

I knew which memory he meant; he had been aboard on the day.

A scatter of small craft showed on the radar, but none of them was our quarry. Angling boats, out for the day. It was more than an hour and a half before we picked up a trace that seemed as if it might be the right craft. He must have been carrying all night to get away that early. His vessel was still beyond the twenty-five-mile ring. Our ship, the Ocean Voyager, had been re-powered, and remodelled fore and aft since my father's time, and could make sixteen knots with a thousand tons aboard. We were in ballast with three of the tanks full: We were getting everything out of her that we could, and we cracked everything on.

He surprised us though, because even though we overhauled him at a rate of knots, it became clear he would make it to the position about twenty minutes ahead of us. The sea was a mirror. Our wake split it and divided it in an ever-widening furrow astern. None of us said anything. Owen Friel's comment, from Conaghan's tape of the time, surfaced in my brain and would not go away:

"There was never a day like it."

Something else was bothering John. A second craft had appeared on screen, astern, and was overhauling us as if we were hove to.

"It must be doing at least fifty knots," he said. "It's been on screen this last half hour, and it will be alongside in twenty minutes."

I lifted a pair of binoculars and went to the boat deck. From habit, I ran my fingers along the side of the wheelhouse, like a blind man feeling his way. My fingers touched the scar in the steel; the scar that had never been healed.

"What ever this is," I prayed, "this is for you, Father!"

I put the glass on the vessel astern. I could see little: A white bow atop an even whiter bow wave: Three dark figures above that, peering ahead, across a raked spray shield.

"Brodie!" I couldn't make out the figures, but it had to be Brodie and his protection.

Then it came to me. There had been two men on the street on the previous day; in the afternoon. I thought them no more than a couple of sight-seers; fishermen I didn't know, who had come to look at the tuna gear. But now that I remembered, they hadn't got near the shed. Owen Friel had intercepted them, and had appeared to be arguing with them.

Tailored suits! How did I not spot them?

It was funny, too, that there had not been a third text-message advert.

I scanned ahead with the glasses. Patrick must have come up on his mark, I thought, because he put the helm over, and a figure on deck fired over the first of the buoy lines. The other fifteen went over in turn, at regular intervals, as the craft came around in a broad circle. About half a mile, I reckoned. Then he headed for centre and came astern, hard.

The two of them were on deck then, and I could see clearly a great cod-end of stuff being hoisted off the deck and swung over the side; then Owen himself hanging over the rail, attaching something – a box, I thought – to the net of stuff in the water.

"Jesus!" I shouted, "The fucking Semtex!"

Just at that moment, he straightened himself back on board and raced for the wheelhouse. Our ship to ship radio crackled. I heard it even on the boat deck:

"Ocean Voyager, Ocean Voyager. Retribution here. Imperative you take way off your vessel, repeat imperative. Have Semtex with trembler detonator over the side. Repeat, have explosive with trembler detonator alongside. Acknowledge!"

None of us knew what name Owen was planning to call his vessel. We only knew that he painted out the old name. But there was no mistaking his voice, or the tone.

John acted on the instant. He killed the throttle, took the pitch back to zero. He shouted at me, but I was already signalling frantically to the fast-craft which was almost level with us by then. They slowed also, in the dramatic way those craft do: When the power is cut, the bow wave collapses and the craft literally sits down into the water.

It was Brodie, with two of his bodyguards. They were unmistakable. Both were wearing sunglasses. They tickled the craft ahead slowly and drew abreast of the 'Retribution'.

In the meantime, Owen Friel had come out on deck again and was lowering away steadily on a blue rope running over the side; then he stopped and belayed a bight of it on the rail. Brodie hailed him, but we were lying too far off to hear the actual words.

Anthony Killoge's father had picked up the tail of the rope that was lying loose about the deck, and started coiling it. It seemed to me that the coils he was making were bigger than might normally be the case, and that he was particularly deliberate in the way he laid the rope, turn after turn into his left hand. When he was done, he handed the coiled rope to Owen, who split it, making two coils of it, and took one in each hand.

The conversation, which had continued all this time, now became agitated. Angry even! The dark-glassed bodyguards each stuck a hand in a pocket. It was an ominous move: Intentionally so.

"Wrong move!" I thought.

Owen reached back his right arm, slowly, then swept it forward in a high, rising throw. At the moment of release, he flung the coil in his left hand in a back handed manner, and the rope snaked out over the gap between the two vessels.

I still have this mental image – there was no photographer this occasion – of the rope hanging in the air in two perfect half hitches.

One of the bodyguards lunged in an attempt to catch the rope, and either tripped or over balanced. The coils dropped neatly over his head.

I have this second image; of a hand snigging the slip knot on the rail of the 'Retribution'.

The rope slapped out over the rail of the 'Retribution'. Brodie, who had caught the tail of the rope, belayed it to the rail of the fast-craft.

"Wrong move again!" I thought.

It was as if some giant fish had turned the tables on our kind. The man with the rope about his neck was snatched out over the side and drawn down into the deep. Some specimen! Almost simultaneously, Friel made a drive for the wheelhouse, and I was conscious of a surge of foam under his stern.

The rope snapped taut on the rail of the Brodie's craft. For one micro mini-second, nothing happened. Then it was as if the entire ocean erupted. A massive column of water shot skywards between Brodie's fast-craft and Owen Friel's vessel. Smoke and foam enveloped the stern of the 'Retribution'.

The shock wave hit the Ocean Voyager like a hammer blow and almost threw us off our feet.

The fast-craft caught it broadside-on, and was catapulted sideways in an almost perfect somersault. Brodie and the second bodyguard were flung clear of the boat and dropped into the ocean somewhere beyond my field of vision.

The body of the first man was vomited up out of the deep. At first it seemed as if he was alive, and waving at us. Then we saw the blue knot at his neck, and the tails of rope trailing from it, and the bulging eyes. He looked like one of those big-scaled, goggle-eyed exotic fishes they trawl up from time to time; and we realised that the limply waving arms betokened a man with every bone in his body broken, and we knew he was dead.

The body fell back into the seething water, into the centre of a steadily widening swirl, and floated there; buoyed up by a red life jacket.

Just then, a second rumbling started. It was something we felt, more than we heard. The deck trembled beneath our feet. The force of the explosion must have driven great bubbles of gas downwards, and now they were escaping to the surface. As each of them broke free in turn, they caused the arm of the dead man to rise and fall, as if he was beckoning to us.

Then, the micro bubbles came. A pinpoint at first, they widened out in a hissing, eerie circle. Where they appeared, buoyancy just didn't exist. The body was the first thing to go. It disappeared before our eyes. We never saw it again. We watched, fascinated, as the fast-craft drifted back in towards the curiously dark circle, and dipped and slid beneath the surface. Only smoke and mist remained; and silence.

As everything cleared, we saw the 'Retribution' coming about hard towards two red life-jacketed figures in the water.

"No-o-o-o O-o-wen, no-o-o-o-o o o."

Martina's cry could have driven nails into steel, so desperate was it!

I don't know yet if he heard it, or if he had already decided not to run them down, but he came astern, and as they washed clear of the side, he gaffed them aboard, none too gently, with a boat hook.

On the eternity of the long steam back to Killybegs, I tried to figure out whose hand it was that snigged the rope at the rail. As near as I could determine, it had the veins of a man old enough to be my grandfather. Anthony Killoge was avenged.

CHAPTER TWENTY FIVE

ALL THE PRETTY FLOWERS

Diary entry, June 16th, 2001.
Jenny Stronnach's journal.

I came back for the funerals. Conaghan insisted: It was work, but it had also become personal. Before that I had covered the search.

I chose not to stay with Mary Katherine and Stephen, and not in any of the local hotels either. It would have been too embarrassing to be with them on a daily basis, even to bump into one of them in the street. As for Ruan: He and I had become just too close. I had lost my perspective. I was ten years older than he was, for chrissakes. It was better I kept away, for the moment. I opted for a bed and breakfast house in the border village of Ballinahown: It was convenient to the search area.

I met Mary Katherine's two brothers, though. At any other time, I would have been thrilled to do so. They were such interesting people. But they weren't the principle subject, and, at first, were slightly out of focus.

They said they were comfortable with the situation, but as I got to know them and they me, they confided that it would not be as easy as Stephen seemed to think. This area was more like Aran: Limestone terrain. Their island, they said, was granite, and their skill was in knowing where the deep pockets of grit lay, and in 'reading' the vegetation on the thin granite soils for traces of disturbance.

The vegetation in this place was altogether more lush, the grass more tussocky. It was a challenge.

They were quick to learn, though. Two small mounds seemed not to fit the general pattern of the landscape, and they had the police searchers excavate them. They came across bones right away; animal bones! Some of the cheaper tabloids mocked them for it, but Starrett took the finds deadly serious. He thought the animals could have been killed to conceal human remains. Conaghan saw it differently. He believed they were probably the bones of animals that died 'naturally', from neglect perhaps, and that they were buried to avoid the attention of knackers, or of agricultural inspectors. Inquisitive intruders would not have been welcome.

"Keep the faith. Stay with it, Jenny," he encouraged me.

I needed that encouragement. The days were fine. I had been through assignments before where the hours were spent just hanging around waiting for something to happen. The evenings, and the nights, were different. I dined alone most nights; sometimes in the almost-too-neat Protestant village of Kesh, just across the border; other evenings in the hotel at Lisnarick. Places that were only a convenient taxi-ride away. I brooded on the whole business I had gotten into, and tried to tally the dead.

Francis, in that terrible death at sea, was the first, Anthony Killoge, the second! The three LRA volunteers – if Owen Friel was to be believed – made five. The two labouring men in the hijacked pick-up truck made seven. Five and seven, two of my 'magic' numbers! Frances Coll, God save us, made eight. Then there was the other woman, another LRA volunteer; I mustn't forget her, she made nine. McMenamy was ten.

Then the news broke of another disaster at sea. An explosion! One man was lost, two saved. Brodie was one of the two. There were few real details. Ruan and Owen Friel were there: Owen in his newly acquired boat: Ruan, along with Martina, on the 'Ocean Voyager'. Nevertheless, I counted the man who was lost as number eleven. Another 'magic' number! Surely that would make an end of it. I was almost satisfied with my reasoning, for no good logical reason, when I remembered Conaghan's boy.

"Twelve! It's not over, yet," I thought, and felt very depressed.

The two brothers were great. Maybe they sensed the disquiet in me; maybe they felt a need themselves for support, but they invited me along with them as they walked and re-walked the land. One of them pointed out a small feature that interested him. He had noticed it, he said, on the very first day he came on the farm; but it was only when he had someone sympathetic, I suppose, to talk to about it, that he decided to investigate further.

"Come and look at it," he said one morning.

It wasn't anything I would have given a second thought to: Three spikes of a tall, leafy plant. They were standing a couple of metres out from a Whitethorn hedge. Two of them were in flower. Pink, bell-shaped flowers that I recognised instantly: Foxgloves!

"Digitalis," he said to me. The seeds must live forever in the soil. It seems to germinate when the ground is disturbed."

"It springs up along the edge of the road," he continued, "where there have been road works. We have seen a lot of it in Donegal."

When it was pointed out like that, the two pink wands, set against the Whitethorn, which was in full bloom, took on an eerie significance.

Just then, he stumbled, almost twisting his ankle. Some unevenness in the ground!

"Thought so," he muttered, "a depression. The ground has sunk."

Then, forgetting I was there:

"Greedy buggers; they've lasted fifteen years. Good nourishment, I suppose."

The implication of what he had said was only just sinking in, when he reached down and caught firm hold of a tussock with his two hands and started tugging on it. First this way, then that: he seemed not to want to rip it out by brute force, rather to loosen it. Finally it came with him. He brushed away some loose earth from what I took to be a large stone.

I was slow. I failed to see what he saw. Where then my famous 'eye' for a camera shot? It was only when he dropped to one knee and swept the hat from his head with his left hand, while simultaneously crossing himself with his right, that it dawned on me. It was a skull he had uncovered.

A skull! I shivered. I couldn't help it

"Thought so," he said again, with evident satisfaction. Then, he jammed the man-of-the-west hat he was wearing firmly back on his head and turned to me.

"You'd better go down and alert the search team. Tell them they won't need the ground-penetrating radar."

When everything was uncovered, Starrett allowed me photograph the opened grave. Clearly two bodies had been interred in it.

Interred! That's too polite a word for it. 'Thrown into' would more nearly describe what must have happened.

The arm of one – well, the bones of the arm – lay across the breast of the second, almost as if the one were still alive when buried, and had tried to protect the other.

The photograph, when published full-page in 'The National Correspondent', raised a storm. Conaghan had printed in sombre black across the top:

LOST….

and underneath:

…. and were FOUND!

It was a triumph for the brothers; they had achieved what was needed. Delaying only long enough to inform Mary Katherine and Stephen, they left for home. The job was done. They wanted no publicity, no more than if one of their own illegal poteen-stills was discovered.

I was glad for Starrett. He put his trust in the family, and was more open than any other senior police officer I ever met. At the same time I was glad not to be him. This was Ireland: A thousand 'dear sir' messages and e-mails hit the letters editor's desk, and the shops and bars echoed with crass opinions too quickly offered and too loudly voiced. Worst of all were the politicians. There were jellyfish statements of support; practised phrases that were like the clinging tendrils of the brown jellyfish that invade the West Coast in summer, a sting in every cell. It was no matter that their utterances would dry and disappear in the light of the truth; they poisoned at the touch.

The Commissioner backed him however; approved a request for a search warrant for the old house, and allowed Starrett bring in the police sub-aqua team. They struck lucky; they discovered a rusting pick-up truck in only the fifth small lake they tried. There was a mess of bones and half-rotted clothing in the cab: The remains of two men. Each skull was pierced by a single concise hole. They – whoever the 'they' were – wasted no ammunition.

I agreed to cover the funerals of the first two. Both female, one had to be Frances Coll, and was quickly established as such. In his attempt to discover the identity of the second, Starrett called in a favour himself. He had Conaghan run a sympathetic piece appealing for the family to come forward. I think it must have been Doyle that wrote it. Conaghan always said Doyle was reliable. The piece opened with a question for our time:

"Was it in Sophocles' play, *Antigone*," he wrote, "that the Gods decreed: *'The living have no business with the dead'*?"

She was a Tyrone woman; young, as one might expect. Her family was never told what befell her; was never allowed the comfort of mourning her until now.

I photographed them from a distance with the biggest lens I could muster. I watched as the mother faced the 'honour party' at the gates of the church. Watched as the mother, a dignified figure in black, waited while the flag, black beret and gloves were removed, then declined to accept them. Watched as the same mother, when the grave had been filled in, walked over to a second mother in black, Mary Katherine!

Throughout the burial, Mary Katherine, with Ruan, Stephen and Martina, stood together at a respectful distance, and made no conversation with anybody, not even themselves. Afterwards, no words were necessary, only a handclasp from one grieving mother to another.

The funeral of Frances Coll was off the scale. Even with the best lens that I had, I captured only part of it. The crowd spilled over into the car park and onto the road outside. Many took to the fields to the back and side of the graveyard in an attempt to be present, to be part of it. But in a real sense, only the family belonged. That is why I thought not to be there. Stephen and Mary Katherine, Ruan and Martina! And for all of the crush, they were given the space to be on their own.

Mary Katherine's brothers came – sisters too, and their families – still with their distinctive men-of-the-west hats jammed onto their heads, and stood as brothers stand on such occasions, not knowing what rightly to do with their hands.

At the graveside, the coffin was allowed rest on timbers that spanned the void in the earth while the family engaged … What was that expression of Ruan's? … in a 'mixed excuse me' of hugs and embraces. Then they made their farewells to the one whom they could not hug, and even Mary Katherine's two brothers bared their heads.

That was the strangest image of all: The pair of them with their pale tonsures and flattened hair, contrasting with their seventy-year, weather-beaten faces.

I captured it all from the height I had marked the day before: Even the normality of the brothers taking the shovels to fill in the grave as the prayers were recited. It was what they would have done on the island.

I was confused: Desolate! Half of me wanted to hide, to similarly obscure myself in the anonymity of doing the job. But ninety per cent of me wanted to go to him, to Ruan. Maybe that was what scared me: It was to him I wanted to go, not to them.

It was Stephen who searched me out. I flustered, not knowing what to say to him, but he drew me to him with an arm about my shoulders.

"Never mind the photographs. Conaghan has had his due. Come with me now. You belong with us."

I cried, for me and for them.

"There," he comforted me. "She's at peace now."

Then we were together with the rest of the family, and with Ruan, and it was easier. But there were things that wouldn't let go of me, even there, and it was as we were leaving the graveyard, by a side gate, that I got the opportunity to ask Stephen:

"That photograph! You know, the school photo, that I was looking at that night …"

I hesitated, not sure how to put it.

"You know … that McMenamy …"

He nodded at me.

"What about it?" he asked.

"There was another girl, taller than some of the others."

He nodded again.

"It was probably ... Maybe ... I'll have a look."

I didn't cover the other two funerals, only attended them. The remains of both men, one married, one single, were buried in the one graveyard on the same day. The attendance was not as big as for Frances' funeral, but took just as long to clear. I saw Owen Friel and Martina standing together in the thick of the crowd, but although they stood there until almost everyone had gone, no family member from either set of mourners spoke to them. There are some things that are beyond forgiveness, I suppose. When the embarrassment became too much for the two of them, they drifted away slowly. I was just about to leave, myself, when I overheard the single daughter of the man who had been married, remark to no one in particular:

"All the pretty flowers!"

CHAPTER TWENTY SIX

FINAL ENTRY

Diary entry, June 22nd, 2001.
Jenny Stronnach's journal.

I came back again for Midsummer's Day. I was invited. Ruan's doing. 'Something special' to show me, he said. I wasn't sure. I drove myself, a borrowed car. Just in case I needed to get away.

I arrived the evening before. A new plank door hung in a freshly painted casement. The 'good Stephen', I guessed. For almost fifty years he was Mary Katherine's leading man; he was bound to have played 'Fluther'.

Inside, the room had been mended, the pane in the window replaced. There was new glass in the framed photo of Martina. The severed hanging lamp was level with its mates again. A new television set, a flat, liquid crystal display of a thing, filled the alcove – 'Digital', Stephen said. It was one of those compensatory things people do for themselves, and I recognised it for such. But it was a quiet room. This new certainty of Frances' death set its own terms. Mary Katherine billeted me in the same guestroom as before: That at least was unchanged.

I woke with the dawn and drew back the curtains to savour the glorious light that flooded in across the hill. It was hours before anyone else rose, even in that house, and I lay there like a child, seeing everything that was to be seen in that room, until I heard the others up and about. Breakfast was leisurely, but I watched the clock, and when it was time, asked Mary Katherine if she would like me to drive her to Mass. We were different faiths, she and I – at least I had been christened into a different Church and I'm sure she knew – and she appreciated the offer.

"That's kind of you," she said.

Ruan stayed. He had sandwiches and coffee to ready - "for the outing" - and was waiting for me when Mary Katherine and I got back from Mass.

"I hope you have good walking shoes," he said, as a reminder.

He had been insistent that I take good shoes, preferably boots, because the hills were rough, and paths uneven.

"Ankles twist easily," he added.

On hills?

That's what I thought of them; hills! Not mountains! There was nothing much above 2200 feet anywhere in the Blue Stacks. But I was out of breath and trailing him long before we made our first halt of the day. He was relentless.

"Laggard!" he mocked me. "We have to be there for midday, remember."

What the hell midday had to do with wherever we were going, he never explained, nor could I remember him doing so previously. I had no problem being taken to the top of his world; was quite willing to be propositioned with a – "all these things will I give you" type of proposition – but it made me mad to be taken so much for granted. He kept driving on. The sun boiled down on us, and I had taken no hat with me. It was so bright it was painful to look at my watch. I figured it very close to midday. The gradient eased, and he led the way into a kind of a defile in a bank ahead of him. I followed, then suddenly emerged in an extraordinary kind of a basin

What was extraordinary about it ….

No! That's not the way to say it. Everything about this place was extraordinary.

I don't know that what happened afterwards was real. I mean, was I hallucinating? The sun too high! Hyperventilating through shortness of breath? I know I filmed part of it with the DV Cam, but there's nothing now to prove it.

We were in a basin, an oasis almost, that was lush beyond anything you could imagine in those bare hills. It was lozenge shaped: A jewel on the neck of the mountain. It was carpeted in a thick green sward. Not a flat green; it was shot through with the incandescent hues of a myriad wildflowers; and it was ringed about with a twist of dwarf, stunted oak trees. I never imagined oaks could grow so high in the mountains, in Ireland.

Ruan was saying something:

"Cahir Crom"!

"This is a special, an ancient place. This is where I wanted to bring you."

But I wasn't listening. I was looking at a great disc of white rock that gleamed in the hillside above the apex of this lozenge, and at the couple that were bathing themselves ...

No, that's not right, either.

    ... that were anointing themselves in a pool a short distance out from the base of the rock. Both were as naked as when they were born.

Ruan hadn't seen them yet. He was reciting his story of that place from an image he had in his head of some previous visit, perhaps his first.

I was scarcely listening. This was the dream that I had, that night in the hotel in Killybegs. One of the bodies was familiar to me. I had run my fingers down the hard ripple of those stomach muscles. My palm had come aflame with the electric tingle of that dark body hair. Owen Friel, as I live and die!

I was as blind to the second person as Ruan was to both. In the dream it was me; then it wasn't. I couldn't see for tears of jealousy. It was me who should have been in that pool with him. But I stopped, and taking the DV Cam from the mini-knapsack I had been carrying on my back, I started filming.

Ruan had, himself, stopped, when he finally looked for real and saw the two intertwined in the pool. It was only then he realised, I was video-ing what was happening, and not in any disinterested way. When I faced him, I wore the same guilty look I faced him with in Donegal Town. I was wearing that same look now. I know it myself. The longing, the lust, was like a knife inside me.

"This is not right," he said, "This is not how this day was intended to be." And he dragged at my arm, pulling me in the direction of another path that led away through the oaks.

"It's not right," I echoed him, still wanting it to be me in the pool, but I kept filming as he kept dragging at me, and it wasn't until we were clear of that profane place that I realised I had wanted Ruan to be in that pool also. And it was only then that I realised whose was the second nude body we saw: Martina's!

I tried to stop again, to return the DV Cam to the backpack, but it was like trying to slig into shoes on the run. Ruan wouldn't stop, so I continued at a trot after him, arguing loudly and berating him for an overgrown pup.

"Jealous of anyone that looks at me!" I taunted him.

"Not those that look at you! It's not those that look at you that bother me; it's those you look at, and the way you look at them. That's what bothers me."

He choked then, and I thought he would say no more, but then the bitterest thing of all:

"Jesus! He's my Godfather, for Christ sake."

That's the way it went, on and on, neither of us yielding to the other. God knows what ground we covered or where we were going.

Funny thing, it was I who started to cry. Funny, because I thought I was the hard one. He moved back towards me to comfort me. The air must have been particularly dry, because I can remember thinking: "I must use a better hair mousse." Then, as we touched, a spark jumped from his outstretched hand to mine.

"Jesus Christ!" he shouted and he threw himself at me and knocked the two of us flying into a bank of bright green ferns. I particularly remember thinking how green they were, and what an asshole he was. My backpack had gone flying, God knows where. Then there was a crack, and I heard the sizzle as the bolt of lightning struck the ground hardly fifty yards away. It was like being hit all over with a hammer in one go. I couldn't breathe. I didn't know that he was any better. The two of us lay there.

I thought I had died; thought, "So this is what it is like." I couldn't see anything, a white light only. There was a pain in my chest. A bullet? I felt at one with Frances and the Tyrone woman. At one and a threesome! Magic numbers! I expected them to take my hands, one either side. I was the thirteenth, unlucky and magic all at the same time; and in all those thirteen deaths, only three of us were women.

But that pain in my chest! One, two three four five. The pain stopped. Then it came again: One, two three, four, five. Something was over my mouth. Death was kissing me, and I couldn't breathe.

"Jenny!"

Somebody was calling me. I wanted to call back, but I couldn't speak. Those lips that kept coming over mine wouldn't let me. I struggled. I trashed about. Death should be pleasant, something welcoming. This was pain. There it was again: One, two, three, four …..

I think it was the rain that revived me. Big, cold drops; big as fifty pence pieces. Cold! So cold it took my breath away and I struggled to inhale. I felt arms around me, lifting me, caressing me. I realised that the reason I couldn't see was that I had my eyes closed. I opened them. I was in the arms of Ruan Coll, and his face was wet against mine, and I never loved him as much. But the rain was real, and as he strained to half-lift, half-drag me to shelter, it turned into a downpour.

This was a dream again; that other dream, the dream I had the afternoon I fell asleep on top of the covers in Mary Katherine's guestroom.

We had been arguing so much, neither of us noticed the clouds building atop the thermals rising from the valley floor, or the blackness of the growing thunder-head, and it was only the realisation that everything about us was crackling with static that made Ruan throw himself at me. Standing on that exposed hillside, we would have been the prime strike-point for the lightning. As it was, it missed us only by an edge of infinity.

The only shelter was an undercut along the scarp of a bank that sheep had scrabbled out for themselves, and that was then carved deeper by storm winds in the depths of winter. When I could speak, I asked Ruan to find my backpack with the DV Cam in it, and at the same time he picked up his own pack with the flask and sandwiches. I was shivering from the cold, and the fear, but he made little of it, saying it was only a blood-sugar thing, and he broke the roughly made sandwiches in two with his hands, and insisted I chew them slowly. What was it about this man? He wasn't much more than a youth, but he had years and insights that could not be reckoned.

I don't know how long the storm lasted. We talked little, only huddled together for warmth, not admitting even to ourselves that it was for comfort. The sky was black, but the hillside was ablaze with the blue light of the flashes that came sometimes as frequently as seven a minute. Even more! Was that the kind of visibility on that tape of Owen Friels, of Anthony Killoge's, I wondered? Phosphorescence triggered by some electronic pulse? We had never seen that tape. I wondered then, had anybody? Was it for real? Did it exist at all? And immediately regretted doing so. Too many had died.

When the storm cleared, we made our way back down the mountain again. The journey took longer than I expected; we had obviously gone much farther than I thought, even beyond the place we had seen Owen and Martina. It was quiet when we reached that place again, just as it was, earlier, when the pair of them were in the pool. But it was deserted now, and we stood to look. There were so many questions I wanted to ask, but my thoughts were scrambled, and I asked nothing. There was something different about it, though. There appeared to be a shaft of some kind standing near where the pool was.

"Jesus!"

That was Ruan. He was staring in unbelief at the clearly ephemeral pillar. I realised it was a swarm of some kind of insects, spiralling about in a great vertical column. Like smoke, but more solid, somehow.

"Midges!" he said. Then he was thoughtful for a moment, and continued: "That must have been where the shaft stood."

"What shaft?" I asked.

"Crom's" he answered. "The 'crooked one'. This was his place. The same Crom whose name Owen Friel spat at O'Hara as testimony to our enduring folk-memory. He was a greedy bugger. He demanded one third of the crops, and one third of the family. And it had to be given, so that he wouldn't take the other two thirds. It was Stephen that told me about him, but he never showed me where the shaft stood."

Before he could say anything else, two more columns of insects took to the wing, then two more again: Five! But that wasn't all. They kept rising in twos. I took out the DV Cam to film the phenomenon, but nothing happened. I tried to replay what I had filmed earlier when Owen and Martina were in the pool, but nothing either. The lightning strike must have fried the memory.

I started to feel apprehensive. The hum from the columns of swarming insects was electrical, almost like that of a great power station. A hundred of these pinprick malignities could take as many bites from you in as many moments. What might a trillion, trillion do? And that bare white pregnant hillside! There were so many questions that could be asked about this place, but none that you really wanted to. The answer might not be to your liking.

The columns of midges kept rising until there were thirteen in all. Ruan was beside himself.

"If only Stephen could see this," he exclaimed. "Crom, and his twelve lesser idols! No wonder we Irish turned Christian; we already had a Christ figure and twelve apostles."

But the sense of foreboding grew too strong. This was a malevolent presence. Something else was going to happen. Maybe it had already happened. I shouted at Ruan:

"Jesus, do you not see it? Somebody else is going to die. That is what this is telling us. Maybe they already have!" And I started to run.

My panic infected Ruan, and although I had raced ahead of him, he quickly caught up with me and took the lead, then settled to a pace that kept him about twenty yards in front. That's how it stayed for the first mile, and the second, and dear knows how many more; but when we came in sight of home, of Mary Katherine and Stephen's home, his own anxiety powered him ahead again.

When we were half a mile off, and in sight of the house, it seemed to me that Stephen put his head out the door briefly, ducked back inside for a few moments, then, re-appeared in full view, waving to us.

"Jesus, Mary, and Joseph!"

Whatever prayer Ruan tried to utter, got no further than that; he hadn't breath enough for the whole of it.

As we got closer still, Stephen tried to call to us. At first, neither of us could hear him, only a fractured sound torn apart by the wind, and muffled by the pounding in our ears. Then a snatch:

"Brodie …"

Brodie what?

Then another snatch:

"At a rally …"

Then, the whole thing repeated:

"Brodie's been shot. At a rally!"

"Oh, Jesus!" I thought. "Oh sweet Jesus, thank you!"

It wasn't that I was thankful that Brodie was dead: I had no feelings for him, no more than if he was a dog. He dealt in death; I thought he deserved to die. I was just so grateful that neither of those two special people, Mary Katherine and Stephen Coll, whom I had come to regard so much, had been harmed. Crom the Crooked One had already exacted too heavy a price from their family: Francis and Frances. Parents I would never meet.

I slowed. Ruan raced on into the house. Stephen waited until I made it as far as him. He must have seen how dishevelled I was, how distressed. But his eyes asked no question, and he waited for me to speak. His hand squeezed my arm. A supportive gesture! This was a man who knew how to communicate without words.

"Was it so bad?" he asked.

"You just couldn't imagine," I blurted out, then I spilled everything: The lightning strike; the storm, Ruan giving me mouth to mouth resuscitation. I told him of the feeling I had that I had died and how I waited for his daughter, Frances, and the Tyrone woman to come to take me to wherever. And I told him of the special place, and of the thirteen columns of midges that Ruan thought marked the idols of the ancient Celts, and of my own obsession with 'magic' numbers, and of the terror I had: That harm had come; either to himself, or to Mary Katherine! But I made no mention of Martina or of Owen Friel.

He drew me into him with that great arm of his and said:

"Come fornenst the house. It's all over."

He was silent a moment, then murmured:

"Crom's place: Cahir Crom! Thirteen columns! Who would have thought it?

Then we went into the house.

Ruan, and Owen Friel and Martina, who were there already, were watching a rerun, frame by frame, of a news item on the television. It was of an event that had obviously been covered 'live'. There was a flash on the screen to say so. It was an LRA rally, somewhere in the North. I missed the exact location. As Stephen and I joined the others, the camera was panning across the crowd. The stop-frame motion gave a peculiarly disjointed feel to the successive images. Figures seated on the platform came into view, each succeeding frame revealing yet one more person. Then a standing figure: Brodie! There was no sound, so we did not hear the shot; only saw the effect as the bullet hit him.

One second he was alive. A microsecond later, the camera had frozen the blur of the bullet at the very moment of impact. In the next frame, his eyes said he knew he had been hit. A few more frames, and it seemed as if his entire spine erupted from his back.

"Exploding bullet!"

How could this man Stephen know such things? Then I remembered he had been at war in his youth.

I looked at the other two men in the company. My two, you might say; I had bedded both of them.

"What do they feel, now?" I wondered. "Is there a difference between killing for revenge and killing to protect someone? What difference if somebody else does it?"

Whatever they felt, their demeanour revealed nothing; they were as unreadable as Stephen himself. If there was satisfaction in it for either of them, it didn't show. But there was a finality in that moment. Payment was complete. The final instalment had been delivered. Who exactly was paid, I still don't know: Payee unknown! I knew Ruan and Owen had taken no active part in it, and yet they were involved! This day's business was just another marker in a two-thousand-year battle. Good versus evil? But what would I know? I think it was then I realised how little we women know of our men: We expect them to do things for us, then, when they do them, we wonder why.

Martina's body language, in contrast, was crystal clear: She sat at Owen Friel's side, her two hands fastened about his upper arm.

Mary Katherine was transfixed, her eyes locked-on to the screen but seeing beyond it.

"A dungeon horrible, on all sides round" she quoted.

It was Owen Friel who ran with the quotation.

"As one great furnace flamed,"

Pausing only a moment, he continued:

" ... yet from those flames
No light, but rather darkness visible ..."

He paused, letting Mary Katherine back in, but she didn't complete the excerpt.

"You finished it then;" she said to him, "the degree, I mean. I often wondered."

Ruan recited the next line:

"Served only to discover sights of woe."

"Paradise Lost!" he said, identifying the poem, then turned polemical, an Irish failing!

"Milton had it wrong, you know: he would have been nearer the mark to write of darkness indivisible. It's in all of us!"

Neither Mary Katherine nor Owen Friel answered him, but I saw in her eye a rerun of the wild pike-stroke that cut down Ernan McMenamy. I noticed that the pike was no longer resting on the two pegs above the cluid.

Then Mary Katherine excused herself and withdrew to the kitchen. She left a parting thought:

"He was some mother's son, you know."

No longer constrained by her goodness, as it were, my professional instinct kicked in. I insisted that Ruan play it again. I watched everything. At one point, a minor detail caught my eye: A flash of brightness on the screen, a woman with blonde hair, very blonde. I asked Ruan to pause it.

"What do you think?" I asked him.

He looked closely. His soft intake of breath was all the answer I needed. Owen Friel peered at the TV as Ruan pointed to the image. I phoned Conaghan, mobile-to-mobile. I got him in the wire room.

"Have you got it on screen?" I asked.

"Use the frame after the moment of impact," I instructed him. "It is the instant between life and death. That's your picture and your headline."

I don't know what reply he made, because I was already dictating my next instruction to him:

"Look in the same frame for a blonde head; a woman; we think it's Alice LaCombre!

"Jesus!"

His profanity echoed from the shell of the mobile. On a whim, I asked him who or what he thought she might be.

"American?"

It was Owen Friel who answered. He had obviously overheard. Couldn't help but.

"Not American," he said. "Eastern block!"

I looked at him. My eyes asked the question.

"Archie Hamill," he explained. "Archie, the barman in the hotel. She couldn't pronounce his name. Not properly! She said it the way the Russian skippers used to say it. When they were buying mackerel. Back in the eighties."

I must still have looked puzzled, so he added:

"Khh … Mr kHamill! That's the way they said it. They couldn't pronounce the 'H'. Neither could she."

Owen and Martina excused themselves after that; said they were going to the town, "to be seen!"

He explained he didn't want to be picked up, "again", for something he didn't do. They both left, but he reappeared briefly about twenty minutes later. He had a videocassette with him, and left it on the table at Stephen's end.

"Maybe you should have this," he said. "I want no more of it."

He did a peculiar thing. He left it standing on its edge. Then he was gone.

Mary Katherine made supper for us. Something light for Stephen and herself: Soup, warmed in the microwave for Ruan and I. Afterwards, and after she had cleared the supper-things, she knelt for prayers.

"We have been neglecting things," she said. We knelt with her.

Stephen recited the first decade, and Mary Katherine marked it for the safe delivery from death of Ruan and I. Her own decade was for Martina and Owen Friel; Ruan's for peace and everlasting joy for his parents. I don't think Mary Katherine expected me to give out a decade, the Rosary not being a prayer of our Church, but I gave it out as good as any of them. I kept my intentions to myself, though. I prayed for me.

After she had gone to bed, the three of us stayed talking at the table for some time. The events of the entire day; everything that had happened, had shaken me profoundly; especially the quivering columns of midges. The first, the biggest of all, was a shaft of pure evil. I asked Stephen about it, how it was he knew so much about such a place.

"Can evil live so long?" I asked him.

"As long as time, itself!" he answered, "if we yield to it."

He paused a moment, then continued speaking:

"We Colls – Friels, too – have been around a long time, from the very dawn of Christianity, maybe even from before that. We stood against the old beliefs, against the barbarity of them."

Ruan turned and looked at me: A long, silent look, almost a stare. I remembered the way he had done so once previously. We sat on a wall at the place he named as Wattle Bridge, and I asked him about his father. He spoke then only with his eyes, just as he did now. I puzzled at the message in them, trying to interpret it.

Stephen saw the puzzlement in my face, and seemed to think it was caused by something else.

"It has another name, you know, and a different association. That place. A very different association! Some call it 'Cluain Daragh'."

He lowered his voice, almost as if he was afraid Mary Katherine might hear.

"People still go to it to perform a fertility ritual. I think there must have been an older cult; a mother goddess, perhaps."

I ventured a translation of the name: 'The oak meadow'.

Stephen nodded.

"That, or a healing place. The trouble is, 'Cluain' has a third meaning: A deception!"

I gave up the puzzling. Nothing was what it seemed anymore. The laws of physics no longer applied. Darkness was as transparent as day. The mid-summer's brightness became as black as night. That, surely, was what this was about. All to do with light and darkness! I rehearsed a half-remembered snippet from the beginning of St. John's gospel – something that was imprinted in an already long-ago Sunday school:

"... *and the darkness did not comprehend it.*"

This was about seeing: Not the things hidden in the depths of the ocean, but the darkness at the core of all our lives that we do not admit to.

Ruan got up and moved towards the stairs. I moved to follow him. Stephen rose and turned towards the door.

"I must check the house is secure," he said, " and I'll do something with this."

He picked up the videocassette.

"I'll put it in the hiding place, down in the room. We can't play it in any case, not any more; only DVD's now!"

Then he half-turned back to me again.

"You know the girl; the face in the photograph; remember; the one you asked about."

I nodded at him.

"Margaret Brennan! That was her name, Margaret. She was a sister of Martin's; a year or two older than him. She married a reporter."
He hesitated just a moment.

"About that time."

"Name of Conaghan?" I volunteered.

"Conaghan, it was!" he confirmed.

I continued on up the stairs. Consciously I wished the treads to be steps out of the past and forward to the future, but for a moment, I doubted that was possible. I wondered if we can ever truly walk on from our past.

A voice, deep inside, was insistent: Not ever! Not from two-thousand-year pagan deities and blood-sacrifice; not from centuries of picking over old injustices; not from that vicious lust for power; not from the winds of war that blow hot and cold as it pleases the great powers that generate them.

Then I remembered that this was Stephen's, and Mary Katherine's house. And Ruan's! His hand reached out for mine at the top of the stairs. It drew me back the wrong way for the guestroom. This would be the third night I would spend in Ruan Coll's room under this roof. I yielded to my own superstitious beliefs. Three! I didn't hesitate. Magic number!

Death on the Deep Edge

A thriller by

Jago Hayden.

If you have enjoyed this book, please tell your friends. And watch out for the sequel: Ruan Coll will be back. The title of his next adventure is:

Death by the Wayside

Also by the same author:

HAIR ALL CURLING GOLD

A memoir of growing up in Co Wicklow in the 1940's and 50's.